The Bird Whistler

By

Ellen M. Rutgers

The Bird Whistler
Ellen M. Rutgers

ISBN: 979-8-9864100-5-0
Published by: Nicasio Press
                 Sebastopol, California
                 www.nicasiopress.com
Cover Design: Will Cosgrove
Font: Dutch Mediaeval Pro

For Alef

Contents

Prologue

1933

With all his might he tried to bring life back into her young and innocent body, holding her hand and whispering sweet words that would have made her smile not even a week ago. The only response he received was a gentle beam of sunlight occasionally dancing through the darkened room. Then there was silence. Long periods of silence, just sitting in the space of death. For the first time, Johnny experienced the feeling inside that comes when faced with the irrevocable fact that someone so dear to you has left forever. His breath became shallow. His eyes stared without seeing as he sat beside his baby sister, motionless.

He didn't hear the opening of the door; he didn't hear the footsteps moving closer to him. He didn't even feel the warm hand resting on his shoulder. Finally, he looked up, and he saw his father's eyes filled with tears, swallowing his grief, and he realized that they shared the same feeling. Love flowed between them. Together they left the room, trying to move on with life.

1943

"When you ring the bell, someone will open the door. They know you are coming," Johnny softly spoke to the six-year-old girl sitting on the back of his bike, who was holding on tightly to his oversized sweater.

"I'm scared."

"Don't be; your parents are safe. You too need to be safe. You'll be together soon."

"What's her name?"

"You can call her Aunt Josie, and remember, Esther, your name is Els, and she is your aunt."

"How much further do we have to go?"

"We're almost there. The next farm."

*   *   *

VanderHaar from the Resistance had told him, "The less you know the better. Just ride your bike, and if they stop you, she is your sister Els."

It was quiet and dark. At this hour nobody dared going out. Johnny knew the road by heart and he didn't need the light on his bike. His night vision was strong enough for him to follow the uneven winding road to the farm on the outskirts of the village.

In the distance he heard the rumblings of an approaching vehicle. Johnny quickly pulled over, pushed his bike behind a bush, and found a hiding spot for both of them, a good ten yards away from the bike. As the sound drew closer, beaming headlights powered through the otherwise peaceful landscape. Their hearts were pounding as the German jeep passed. They waited for what seemed hours before Johnny decided it was safe to continue their journey through the night.

"We're almost there, don't be afraid," Johnny tried to calm Els, one hand steering his bike, the other reaching back to hold onto Els, as though this gesture could prevent any further calamities.

He stopped his bike and helped her get off.

"I'll wait here till you are in safely. Just go to the door and ring the bell. Aunt Josie will open the door for you. She will say, 'Hi Els, my dear niece, I'm so glad you are here.' That means you can trust her, and you can go in. If you don't hear those exact words, you apologize. Say you are at the wrong door, then come back to me quickly. You are Els from now on, and she is your Aunt Josie. Be safe!"

"Thank you," Els whispered with a small trembling voice.

"Go now, be strong."

Johnny waited back behind a bush while Els walked up the narrow path leading to the front door of the farmhouse. A small bag with few of her belongings was hanging over her shoulder. Not long after she had pressed the bell, the door opened.

"Hi Els, my dear niece, I'm so glad you are here."

Els went in, the door closed, and Johnny jumped on his bike and rode as fast as he could back home. For a few miles the waxing moon cast a faint shadow of his silhouette riding his bike on the dirt road. His village seemed fast asleep. But in the schoolhouse in the center of the small town, a dim light gave away that his father and mother were still up waiting for his safe return.

Though they didn't know the specifics of Johnny's nightly bike rides, they knew about his involvement with the Resistance. Johnny wouldn't tell them anything. As VanderHaar had told him, "The less anyone knows the better." No questions were asked, but both his parents hugged him every time he came home safely.

"Thank God, you made it," his mother said softly.

So far Johnny had been very successful with his nightly adventures. VanderHaar, who was heading the network in the Resistance, had come to trust him and used Johnny for the most challenging missions. Johnny didn't question his own participation in the Resistance. No one stopped him. It was the right thing to do. Even though the school next door, his father's school, was occupied by a group of German soldiers, it didn't stop him from supporting the Resistance Movement.

That night, it was hard for Johnny to fall asleep. The instructions he had received for tomorrow's mission kept repeating themselves, as if to make sure he would not forget. VanderHaar had talked to him about getting the children from Amsterdam. He had the address, and VanderHaar himself would give him a ride to the city. Once in the city, he would take a bicycle to the house on the Prinsen Gracht and pick up a four-year-old boy, Eli. Then he would bike Eli to Amstelveen, a town just outside of Amsterdam. VanderHaar had the false identity papers ready. Eli, now Ari, would be his brother. His own name would be Buter. VanderHaar said it was best to go by a false name, should they be caught. In his mind, Johnny pictured the whole day. Finally sleep took over, much needed to ensure he had enough energy for the next day.

*   *   *

He left the house early, before dawn, while everyone was still asleep. It would be too dangerous for anyone to know what he was up to today. He walked a few miles to the mill near the stream where he was to meet with VanderHaar. The fresh morning air and the slow rising of the sun gave him a sense of freedom. Johnny knew he was doing the right thing, but he also knew he loved adventure. He was courageous for sure, like VanderHaar who followed his calling to help the Jewish children. He wanted to save as many children as he could. So far he had been successful with his endeavors. He had a strong network within the Resistance throughout the country, but it was vulnerable. One wrong person, and the chain would break...

"Good morning," VanderHaar welcomed Johnny at their secret meeting spot. "Let's go before it is too late." Simultaneously they opened the doors of the unassuming black Volvo. VanderHaar started the car, pressed the gas, and gently shifted gears until they were going full speed on the road to Amsterdam. They took the back roads to avoid being stopped by the German soldiers. As they were driving, VanderHaar explained the whole situation.

"When you get to the street, park your bike against the window of the bakery at the corner. You can't miss it. Walk to number one hundred and twenty-eight and ring two times. One long and one short. Whoever opens the door will say, 'Hello Buter, you've come with the bread.' It doesn't make sense but that is the password. No password, no pick-up. You walk away and say, 'Sorry, wrong address.' Make sure you come right back. I'll be waiting for you."

Johnny was used to identifying himself with a password, and so far, it had always worked. Just now he felt a twitch in his stomach, but he kept quiet.

"When you get Eli, you take him to his new address. You know how to go from there."

Johnny nodded. He had rehearsed it in his mind so many times. Though he had not been in Amsterdam before, the description of the streets and the directions by VanderHaar had been very clear. VanderHaar lit a cigarette. He too tried to maintain his calm, but he knew that this was a dangerous undertaking.

They entered the city. VanderHaar parked alongside the road, just as they crossed a bridge. The bike was waiting for him. VanderHaar had arranged for that. VanderHaar would wait, in case something went wrong. Should Johnny drop Eli off, he would pick Johnny up a block away from the house where Eli would hide. He had it carefully planned out.

Johnny stepped out of the car and switched to the bike. He had to hurry. He wanted to be there early, get it over and done with. He followed the directions VanderHaar had given him. The streets in the city were different from the country roads in the rural village where he lived. But no time to think about that. Focus on the job ahead. He entered the center of the city. The houses on the canals were just like he imagined. Prinsen Gracht, yes, the corner, the bakery. It was all there. He leaned his bike against the bakery window. There were hardly any people on the street. It was a quiet morning. The city had not yet come alive. Johnny walked past the houses, one hundred eighteen, one hundred twenty, one hundred twenty-two, until he saw the number sign "one hundred twenty-eight" in curly gold-plated letters. He placed his finger on the doorbell and pushed, one long and one short ring.

He waited. His breath became shallow. He heard footsteps approaching behind the closed door. He was anxious to take Eli with him, and bring him to his safe address. It took a while before the door opened.

"Good morning, how can I help you?"

Johnny's heart skipped a beat. He looked into the eyes of the man in front of him. He was waiting for the password, but nothing happened.

"I-I must be at the wrong place," he heard himself stumble.

"Can I help you?" the man asked with a penetrating look.

"No, No, I'm sorry," Johnny said as he turned back toward his bike. He could feel the man's piercing eyes following him. He didn't dare look back. The block he had walked only a few moments ago seemed to last forever as he set one trembling foot in front of the other. Just when he reached his bike, still leaning against the bakery window, a green German jeep pulled up. Two soldiers jumped out, slammed the doors, and went into the house on number one hundred and twenty-eight. Johnny froze. It didn't take long before a little boy was taken out and pushed into the car.

"*Schnell bitte!*" the harsh voices cut through the early morning silence.

That must have been Eli. Even more children followed. Johnny couldn't just stand there with his bike. They would wonder what he was doing. He pushed the bakery door. Thank God, it was open; he pretended to buy a roll. The guy behind the counter didn't say anything. Neither did Johnny. He just looked intensely at the rolls. His heart was still pounding. An uncomfortable feeling of being caught arose.

Was this baker a betrayer too? Did he suspect Johnny's role in the plan that now had failed?

Finally, the baker broke the silence.

"What do you want?"

Johnny took a roll and placed some guilders on the counter. The jeep outside pulled up and passed the bakery, the screeching sound of tires burning the pavement of the street. Both Johnny and the baker followed the children in the back of the jeep with their eyes. Johnny caught a glimpse of the young boy. Eli? A young, innocent face with sad, hollow eyes, as though asking him, "where were you?" These eyes would be forever imprinted in Johnny's heart. This question would continue to reverberate within him. "Where were you, where were you?"

Johnny looked at the baker. The baker's eyes were filled with disgust and disbelief. No words were needed.

The baker grabbed a basket from behind the counter and filled it with freshly baked rolls.

"Take it," he said, "and be careful."

Johnny took the basket, jumped on his bike, and rode back to the meeting point where VanderHaar was still waiting. He threw his bike to the ground, got in the car, slammed the door, and cried. VanderHaar let him cry.

"We missed. We have to be careful, because there must be a betrayer in the network. We have to be extremely careful," he cried.

After a while, Johnny told VanderHaar everything. He pulled out the rolls the baker had given him. Did VanderHaar know the baker? No, but Johnny was lucky not to get caught.

This no longer was the kind of adventure Johnny could secretly enjoy. His heart was filled with sorrow. Where did the children go? What would happen to them? Were the stories they heard about the camps true? He felt his jaw tighten.

"We must continue these missions," he told VanderHaar.

"We will," VanderHaar replied.

*   *   *

The same back roads took them home, safely once again.

A knock on the door. Two young German soldiers from the school next door politely ask if they could come in. Mother lets them, gives them coffee, and lets them do the talking. German mumble jumble, not the harsh sounds from this morning, just two lonely guys, perhaps nineteen years old, a few years older than Johnny, missing their family. Franz and Albert.

AMSTERDAM

"It's too late to go to America, we have to go into hiding. Mother is in jail. She hasn't even seen Robbie. It is extremely dangerous right now. We must leave."

Edith was pleading with Mark to get him to listen to the warnings that have been given to all the Jewish people on their block. Soon there would be a round-up, and everyone would be taken, just like they were in many of the other neighborhoods.

Robbie was born at home only a few weeks ago. Doctor Polak came over to make sure everything was fine. Luckily there were no complications, and Edith quickly got her strength back. Doctor Polak was also a well-loved family friend. He managed to get into the prison and speak with Sarah, Edith's mother. She wanted to know everything about Robbie. For months she had been embroidering a small blanket and at last she stitched his name in the blanket with colorful silk. She managed to take it with her to jail and was able to give it to Doctor Polak to give to Edith as her gift for Robbie. The future was uncertain, and she was glad that she was able to give her grandson a tangible memory, perhaps the only memory, as a way of blessing him and welcoming him into the world.

Late that night, Doctor Polak went over to the home of Edith and Mark. It was a brief visit in which he handed Edith the blanket for Robbie. He also let them know that if they would be ready the next morning, Truus, a woman from the Resistance, would be able to take them to a hiding place with a couple in Utrecht. They had to make up their mind and they quickly agreed; Edith and Mark packed their most precious belongings, so that they all fit into just two suitcases. After feeding Robbie, Edith wrapped him in the soft protective blanket that Sarah had made with so much love. Everything went so fast. There was no time to say goodbye; there was no time to realize that their farewell could easily be a farewell forever. Edith didn't want to let these thoughts enter her mind. All she could think of was getting ready for the journey very early the next morning.

Truus arrived exactly on time. It was still dark. Edith carried Robbie in her arms wrapped in soft colorful embroidery, and Mark was carrying the heavy suitcases. No one spoke; they quickly got into the car, and Truus pulled out of the street, out of their neighborhood, out of the city, onto the long straight road leading them to their new address. Robbie was well fed and quiet. Though only a few hours from the capital, the ride seemed to last forever. There was tension in the car; too many unknowns. If only they had moved to America when it was still possible! Now they were dependent on the goodwill of other people, brave people, who were willing to risk their lives in order to save them.

The car stopped in front of a villa. The house stood on its own, surrounded by a large yard that seemed to be well-cared for. Truus opened the car doors and led the family to the front door.

"Come in," Nelly smiled as she kindly welcomed her guests to their new temporary home.

"My name is Nelly, and this is my husband Kees. We built a small room in the attic in such a way that no one would ever know people are living there. But be careful with the lights at night, and when you are in the house, stay away from the windows."

Nelly showed them the little space you could only enter by pulling down the stairs from the ceiling, and more or less crawl up. When the stairs were pulled up, there was just a ceiling; nothing that indicated an entrance to the small attic room. Nelly apologized for not being able to provide more comfort, but Robbie didn't seem to be bothered by it, as he was fast asleep in his new soft little bed, prepared by Nelly the day before.

During the day, Kees was mostly in his office downtown. Nelly was home and soon became close to her new guests. Mark had brought a large sum of cash, so he was able to pay for their cost of living. Kees had to spread out his grocery shopping so that no one would be suspicious because of the large amounts of food he was getting. Time was passing. The war raged on. The Germans became more and more relentless in their eradication of Jewish people. Especially in Amsterdam, whole neighborhoods were searched, and the Jews that had not moved away were now being ordered to go on transport to the camps. That's all Edith and Mark knew. They hadn't heard from Mother; neither had they heard from Doctor Polak.

Weeks went by. Even though they lived in fear for their lives, the harmony between them and watching Robbie's innocence, the joy of simple household tasks, gave their lives a dimension they had thus far not been aware of. The simplicity of their daily routines and the experience of shelter amidst all the danger offered a unique opportunity for gratitude to be alive and to be safe.

Safe? One night a car pulled up. Nelly was the first one to hear it.

"Quickly, go upstairs."

Edith went first. Holding on tightly to Robbie, Edith managed to be up in seconds. Nelly cleared the kitchen table. Mark followed Edith, and Kees shoved the stairs up and closed the ceiling off. It all happened so fast, as though they had rehearsed it many times. The bell kept ringing.

Loud voices, German voices. Nelly opened the door, acting surprised at their visit.

She pretended not to speak nor understand German. They didn't bother anyway. They entered the house as though they owned it and searched through every room, opening cabinets, drawers, pulling out papers and precious belongings. Kees stood back trying to keep a straight face while his heart was boiling. Upstairs it was quiet. Edith and Mark held each other tightly. Robbie was sleeping. One sound and they would have given away their hiding spot. Instead the Germans went downstairs to the basement. Waving their flashlights, they expected to find what they were looking for. Besides some old furniture, there were some bags of potatoes.

"Ein Radio, hast du ein Radio?"

Mark shook his head no. They kept only a small radio in the attic, since the new law was established that no one could own a radio, let alone listen to the news that came from England.

The Germans seemed to be in a rush, and when it was clear to them that there was nothing to find, they left the house. Without any apology, they walked out as quickly and as loudly as they had entered the house half an hour earlier.

SEPARATION

That evening at dinner, Edith and Mark were told that they could no longer stay at the house, especially not with Robbie. Edith turned white. She pressed her nails into her palms, looking for sensible words to reply to what she just heard Kees say in his matter-of-fact fashion that served him well in his office, but here lacked every sense of empathy.

"We called Truus, the same woman who brought you here," Kees explained. "If you agree, she will come and pick up Robbie. She knows of a safe address for him back in Amsterdam. She will find a new place for you both and bring you together once everything is settled. She is still working on it."

A tense silence filled the room. Edith slowly composed herself, realizing the danger her hosts were exposed to. She pushed herself out of her chair and slowly walked over to Nelly, her hand gently resting on Nelly's shoulder.

"Thank you for everything. Let's remember the wonderful times we had. Let's remember our conversations. We will always remember what you did for us."

Nelly rose and, like a sister, embraced Edith until Kees continued to deliver his information.

"Truus will come by tomorrow and let you know what she has found. Truly, believe us, we want you to be safe. It is no longer safe here," he tried to justify his decision.

Edith and Mark hugged their friends. They fully understood the danger they were all under at this time. And time was running out.

Edith went upstairs. She took Robbie in her arms and held him tightly to her chest, stroking his little body, caressing his soft black hair. Mark joined her. All night she sat there with Robbie close to her, whispering comforting words, assuring him they would be back together soon. She spoke to him as though he could understand every word she whispered.

"Know that we love you."

"Know that this is only for a few days."

Robbie slept through the night in the safe embrace of his mother's arms.

Edith and Mark stayed awake the entire night, holding on to each other, not knowing what the future would bring.

*   *   *

Truus came early in the morning. She acted calm and spoke reassuringly.

"I found a place in Amsterdam for Robbie. I can take him first. I'll come and get you as soon as I have checked on the other house. If all goes according to plan you should be together within a week."

Edith had wrapped Robbie in his soft protecting blanket. She gently kissed him on his head, before handing him over to Truus.

"I'll be back soon. Know that this is for everyone's safety. Trust me. You'll be together soon."

Edith nodded and forced a smile, as she tried to push the tears inward, not to give away the immense pain of separation she was feeling.

Mark stood there motionless.

Nelly walked Truus to her car and helped Robbie be comfortable on the front seat covered under an old, unsuspicious blanket.

Edith glued her ears to the sound of the starting motor, which quickly faded away into the far distance, into the unknown.

Nelly brought water to a boil and poured the hot steaming water over the scarce ground coffee, filling the room with a comforting aroma.

"I'm sorry." She tried to ease the situation, knowing there really were no words; her awkward apology made no sense. With a trembling hand, she poured the coffee.

They sat together in silence at the kitchen table.

"It's not your fault," Edith said, putting her arm around Nelly. "You've done what you could."

It was a long day, with little or nothing to do, now that Robbie was gone. Mark tried to read, and Edith helped Nelly with the household chores. She tried to catch up on her sleep, and later in the afternoon, she joined Nelly in cooking a meal for dinner.

At the end of the day, not long after dinner, a car pulled up. Edith and Mark rushed upstairs again. Nelly lingered, making sure there was no trace of visitors before she finally opened the door.

It was Truus.

"What happened? Is everything okay?"

"I need to speak to Edith and Mark."

Kees pulled down the stairs, letting them know that it was safe to come down.

They were surprised to see Truus. She looked different from this morning. Her eyes were red, and her calm was a mere façade, trying to hide what she had witnessed that day.

She gathered her courage and began to speak slowly.

"The house, the Germans, they were there before we got there. Someone betrayed us. Kids were taken," she stumbled.

"And Robbie?"

"I gave him to a friend who was going north. He promised to find a place for him and get back in touch with me."

"Where is he now?"

"We don't know, we might not know for a while. I'm so sorry."

A NEW FAMILY

Truus had kept her word. Two days later she had found a family in Amsterdam who was willing to hide Edith and Mark. They had lived in a daze, going through the motions, not really present, and not being able to truly feel their immense loss.

Truus had told them about the new family, a young couple and a baby boy. Fate had it that this boy too was named Robbie. Edith and Mark had decided not to talk about their own Robbie. Should Truus find him, she would certainly find a way to rejoin them.

Henk and Agnes, their new hosts, were welcoming and had created a rather comfortable space on the second floor and a hiding room in the attic, should they receive a visit from unwelcome visitors. The house was big enough to give each couple privacy. Its high ceilings, tall windows, and dark wood floors gave it a solemn impression. A table and two chairs, a white painted steel bed with a curved post, a homemade crochet bedspread, and a small built-in sink reflected the starkness with which Agnes led her life. Everything was neat and organized, without any extras. Edith and Mark stored their few belongings in the attic, using only what was needed in their guest room.

When the families were together, Henk usually filled the room with his warm, charismatic personality. He was a new schoolteacher and had found a job right after college. He loved his work and was often talking about his students. Agnes, on the other hand, soon lost her welcoming façade and before long, her need to control and command the people around her took over. Though Henk ruled in his classroom, at home he was a mere subject to his wife's regimen. She had high standards and easily looked down on those who did not share those standards with her. Maybe it was the ever-so-slight trace of nobility that still ran through her blood, or maybe it was the fact that her father was a well-respected specialist at the University hospital, but Agnes had an air that made you feel inferior in her presence. To her credit though, she did have a strong sense of justice, and if she could help Jews, she would. She did not resist Henk when he came home telling her that he felt it was his duty to hide Jewish people. Their big house could easily be shared. Agnes agreed and could use the help now that her son Robbie was born. Growing up, she was used to having servants in the house, but Henk's beginning teacher salary could barely pay off the mortgage, so she had to do her own household chores. Mark and Edith were able to supplement their meager income and according to her expectation, they would certainly express their gratitude in helping the household run smoothly. After all, Agnes thought, she and Henk were putting their lives on the line.

Mark spent most of his days reading. Henk had an extensive library in which it was not hard for Mark to find a good read to pass time. Edith tried to find her place in this big house. She looked forward to the dinners when Henk would bring stories home from the outside world; a world that she no longer could participate in, a world that rejected her. She was thinking of Robbie, and of her mother. She kept talking to them quietly in her head. She kept imagining that they could hear her and feel her love. Sometimes she imagined hearing them talk back to her. A warm feeling filled her chest when she could hear them in her heart. Then there were other times that she was doing nothing. Agnes had asked her to help with the chores and to take care of Robbie from time to time. She did, yet she never told Agnes about her own Robbie. Sometimes she would shrink inside by the commanding tone with which Agnes made her requests.

"How much longer will this continue?" she thought over and over again, hoping for a sign of the end of the war. But the news that Henk brought home was somber. Even at his school, children were disappearing, and there too they had a round-up to take the few brave Jewish children who were still attending.

One day they overheard an argument between Henk and Agnes. Mark could not help but listen.

"You should not have taken that radio home," Agnes yelled at him. "What if they get wind of the fact that you got yourself that radio. How do you know they are not going to turn you in? How do you know it wasn't a trap?"

"Stop it, Agnes, please," he tried to calm her. "I know what I am doing. We must listen to England. We must know what is going on. We will listen to it upstairs; no one will notice."

"Aren't we in enough danger as it is?" Agnes's fear and desperation cut through the walls, as Mark and Edith were listening in on this conversation.

"What about our baby? We can't take any more risks!"

Henk was surprisingly calm and spoke to her in a strong determined tone.

"Agnes, I understand your fears, but we made a choice, and we will not sacrifice our values for our fears." Henk made an impression on Agnes. For the first time, Edith and Mark realized that Agnes was not always the one waving the scepter at home. They realized that Agnes lived under tremendous fear, wanting to protect her baby. They felt deep compassion, thinking of their own Robbie, their own loss. They decided to live with Agnes, accepting her the way she was, and to try not to let it get to them but instead to cope till this war would be finally over.

EAST OF HOLLAND

"Jerry needs to go to the farm. The Germans will surely come and get him to work for them in Germany. I will not have it that he goes to work in a gun factory. Johnny, go visit with Dora on the farm and see if she is willing to hide him."

"Yes, Dad, I'll do that this afternoon. I was going over there anyway. I'm sure they will have a place for Jerry. There are more guys over there. They work on the farm, and one time when the Germans came to look for young men, the guys were hiding in a haystack or in the pig stable. The Nazis are so squeamish, they wouldn't step foot in there. Should be no problem."

Looking at his older brother, he added, "Besides, Dora's coffee is the best."

Jerry had a bewildered look on his face; anything outside of his comfort zone threw him off. So far he had been able to finish his high school, and his dream was to go to university to study law. Perhaps he could take some books over to the farm, so at least he could prepare for his entry exam.

"Joop, are you still playing chess with those guys next door?" Johnny asked his younger brother, changing the subject. Franz and Albert had become regular houseguests, clearly enjoying the warmth of the large family, the delicious food, and the endless games of chess. Joop was only twelve. He had always been a master at chess, and Franz and Albert were his willing students. Joop also knew a fair bit of German, but he was smart not to let them know. Johnny had clearly instructed him to listen carefully to their conversations. If anything suspicious was discussed, he should tell Johnny immediately. Joop was proud to be able to help his older brother in the Resistance. He didn't know what Johnny was up to, but he did know that Johnny was out there trying to undermine the Germans.

Sometimes Joop went over to the school next door, where eight German soldiers were quartered. Sometimes they wore their uniforms. Their tall shiny boots and their clearly visible guns gave them an air of superiority, and they could easily fill you with fear. But they didn't think much of Joop. Being short for his age, they really only regarded him as the little kid from next door. He was playing chess and didn't understand a word they were saying. But Joop listened carefully to their conversations. So far nothing was revealed in Joop's presence, but Johnny insisted that he keep going there and continue to carefully listen to what they were talking about. Joop actually liked Franz and Albert. They were young, and they didn't seem like soldiers, even though they were wearing a uniform. Mother liked them too. She always fed them, just like she fed the whole family. Johnny had asked her once why she was giving them so much attention. She said not to judge these guys.

"They are kids, just like you and Jerry, and they miss their home. They don't want to be in this war," his mother said as she tried to justify her affection for these guys, whom she knew were the enemy.

"Just be careful, Mom. A lot is happening here, and you don't want them to become suspicious."

His mother looked at Johnny lovingly. How could her son think that she would give away clues about their participation in the Resistance? Secretly she was proud of her children. At first, when she heard that Mara was also helping Johnny, she was struck with fear, but Mara was clear that she had to help. Now that Jerry would go into hiding, and Johnny and Mara in and out on dangerous missions of which she had no clue, she only had Anna and Joop at home. At least Father's older boys, her stepchildren, were safe; one, following in his father's footsteps, was teaching at a school in Amsterdam, and one was already in the States. But the worries of the war began wearing her out. The radio news was not hopeful; it didn't look that the end was in sight. Instead, the Germans gained more and more ground. Also, the rumors about what happened in the concentration camps were gruesome. When Johnny would come home late at night, or sometimes when he would even stay away for a while, her thoughts were filled with what could have happened.

*　　*　　*

"I'm on my way to Dora's farm." Johnny left the house and swiftly jumped on his bike. It didn't take him long before he reached the fields with blooming heather, lush green bushes, and the slightly rolling earth, giving him just enough momentum to take on the next hill. In the distance he saw the farm. He checked to see if he was still alone, and when he realized that no one was around, he began paddling as fast as he could straight to the farmhouse. He put his bike in the little shed that was linked to the main house. He knocked on the door, which led into the large kitchen, where he could smell the aroma of coffee and baked goods. Dora came into the kitchen.

"You frightened us; we didn't know it was you," she said with a quasi-angry tone in her voice. "Next time, give us a sign it's you."

Johnny whistled through his fingers, imitating one of the local birds.

"That's better," Dora smiled, as she was beating up steaming hot milk to pour over his coffee. "What brings you here, besides my coffee?" she said, topping off his coffee with the foam of the creamy milk, fresh from the cow.

Johnny took his mug and slowly began sipping from the delicious warming drink.

"Mom is asking if you can hide Jerry."

"What is happening with Jerry?" Dora asked. "Are they after him?"

"All boys his age are being sent to Germany to work for them. We heard they have to help make guns, working in the factories."

"What about his school?"

"That has to wait, Dora. He will probably bring his books. Don't count on him working on the field or helping with the cows. He is just not that kind of person."

"All right then, one more man in the haystacks won't matter. It has been a great hiding place. It is unbelievable that Camp Erika is just a few miles down the road."

"Do you know what happens in Camp Erika, Dora?" Johnny asked with a tremble of fear in his voice.

"It's the camp for those who refuse to work for the Germans," Dora knew. "I don't know much, but rumor goes that it is brutal in there."

"Are there Jews in there?"

"Not sure. I don't think so; mostly our people, so be very careful."

"So, Jerry can come?"

"Of course."

Johnny gave her a big hug and thanked her.

"Now you be careful, I'm running out of hiding places," Dora joked, but with a serious look on her face.

It was early evening. The rising moon was hanging low over the horizon. Johnny was returning home, steering his bike along the winding narrow path. His heart was filled with gratitude for people like Dora, whose faith was stronger than her fear. She was an inspiration for him. He couldn't wait to bring the news home that it was all right for Jerry to hide at the farm. The thought of Jerry in Camp Erika made him uncomfortable. He looked around. There was no one to be seen. He doubled his speed, eager to share the good news.

ANOTHER DANGEROUS MISSION

"VanderHaar wants to see you," Mara spoke softly to Johnny. Mara was the messenger, and Johnny knew not to question her information. She had been an invaluable link of communication between them all. He kept thinking of her as his little sister, but as he saw the wisdom in her eyes and heard the determination in her voice, he realized that, though still a child, this war had made her grow up fast.

"What time?"

"Eight in the morning, by the mill."

"Thanks, Mara."

He admired his sister's courage. She was a major player and made contact between the different members of the Resistance possible. The Germans wouldn't suspect her. She was a young schoolgirl. She often biked around with a bag filled with schoolbooks on her shoulder. Her innocent appearance would never raise any suspicion that she might be carrying pamphlets, bullets, or even hand grenades in the bags on either side of the back wheel of her bike. Her new name was Mansie, just as his name became Buter. Joop too was starting to play a part in the network, and he was called the young Buter, a name he proudly carried, because he looked up to his big brother.

Johnny hung around longer than usual in the company of his parents, brothers, and sisters, as though he knew that moments like this would become rare in the months, maybe even years to come.

"Jerry, can you bike to Dora's farm?" I'll bring you your stuff later. You can use my bike."

"Can you go with me?"

Johnny didn't want to let his brother down, but he had to meet VanderHaar, and he could not tell anyone.

"You'll be safer if you go alone. I've done it many times. They don't suspect a biker alone. Just go. I'll bring you your books soon."

Mom and Dad nodded, agreeing with Johnny. The rest of the evening was spent in casual conversation and unspoken affection, while drinking hot beverages and staying warm.

Johnny finally walked up the wooden stairs and entered his small familiar room. Lying in bed his eyes scanned around, as though he felt he would not be here for a long time. His clothes were draped over the one chair that was supposed to match his desk and set up for him to focus on his schoolwork. For a long time, he stared at the one photo he loved so much. It must have been about sixteen years ago. He was two and sat on his father's lap. Mother had the two sisters, and Jerry was standing next to his dad. Joop wasn't even born yet, and neither was Swan. A deep sadness overcame him when he thought of Swan. How he loved his little sister, and how he couldn't understand why she died so suddenly. For a moment, he wished he could be that young boy once again, without worries, in the playful safety of his father's lap. He felt his eyelids become heavy, turned off his lamp, and drifted into a realm where life was safe, and Swan was alive.

"Johnny, don't worry about me," Swan spoke to him with a clear and soft voice. She looked at him with deep brown, loving eyes. "Trust, Johnny, do what you have to do, and don't worry, trust." He felt so connected with this little being of light and reached out to embrace her etheric body. She smiled and then slowly disappeared into the dark velvety-black night.

The dream woke him up. He sat up straight in his bed, trying to recall every moment of what he had just experienced in his sleep. "Don't worry, trust, do what you have to do." The words still echoed in his mind. "How could Swan know?" "Where was she?" He gave up trying to understand. He also decided not to share his dream with anyone else but to keep this experience deeply hidden in his heart. He knew that nobody would take him seriously. He also knew that he could follow the message he received from his little sister who he had loved so much and had to part with so long ago. A sense of lightness filled him as he embraced his pillow and fell into a deep, restful sleep.

The following morning breakfast was served early. Mother had set the table with freshly baked bread, cheese, ham, and hot coffee. Johnny ate all he could and was in a rush to get to the mill. Before he left, he slapped Jerry on the shoulder.

"See you soon, bud. You're lucky, you'll have breakfasts like this every day. Safe ride. I'll get you your books by the end of this week."

Jerry gave him a wry smile.

"Thanks, Johnny"

Johnny had a long walk ahead that morning. Jerry was using his bicycle, so he had to walk. It was seven; he had an hour to get to the mill. He looked like an ordinary schoolboy, yet it was somewhat suspicious to be out this early. He was careful not to be noticed. Mother had packed some sandwiches and a thermos with hot coffee in his schoolbag. He carried his identity papers in his pocket. Without the papers, he would be at a loss. Jerry must be riding his bike to the farm now. He felt sorry for his brother. He knew his fears. Jerry had always been different from him. Jerry loved books, and school was his life. For Johnny, the war was a welcome relief from the endless evenings of studying different languages and history. He couldn't get himself to do it, considered it a waste of time. Math and science, on the other hand, came easily to him. But best of all he liked to mess with things that were broken, trying to fix them. Not a skill that was appreciated at school, but for the first time welcomed when he was able to fix the one and only radio they owned this spring, so mom and dad could listen to Radio Oranje or to the BBC. Life was upside down, and though he enjoyed not having to deal with school, he'd never wanted a war to make this happen.

He passed the streets with the houses on either side and entered the asphalt path that led to the stream and the dike. He hadn't seen a soul and was glad that in just about fifteen minutes he would see VanderHaar. With a mix of anxiety and curiosity, he anticipated hearing what today's mission had in store for him.

Before long he saw the familiar car that VanderHaar drove when they went to Amsterdam. VanderHaar was waiting for him, smoking a cigarette.

"Wanna smoke?"

Johnny hesitated, but VanderHaar seemed to think it was okay.

"It calms the nerves, Johnny. We'll need it today. Get in the car, and we'll drive, so we won't draw attention to us should some Nazi be roaming the area."

Johnny lit his first cigarette. It felt like an initiation. Just like he noticed only last night that Mara was no longer a young girl, today he felt he was initiated in a task only a man would take on. He couldn't tell whether he liked the cigarette or not, and tried to copy VanderHaar, drawing the smoke deep into his lungs, followed by a nasty coughing fit.

"Easy, Johnny, don't start off taking in all the smoke. Just a little is enough; the rest can come out of your nose without even getting through the lungs."

Johnny was grateful for this advice and actually enjoyed the motions of smoking a cigarette.

They drove for a while. Then VanderHaar pulled over. He pulled out a bag of tobacco.

"Let me teach you how to roll your own, Johnny. They are a lot cheaper and easier to get."

He took out a thin small piece of paper and carefully spread out the tobacco evenly across. Then he skillfully held it between his index finger and his thumb, using the other fingers to roll the paper down into a small, white, cone-like shape, what looked like a crooked cigarette.

"Try a couple and see how it goes." As VanderHaar was driving again, Johnny practiced rolling his own cigarettes, and pretty soon he got the hang of it.

"How's it going?" VanderHaar asked with a fatherly tone in his voice.

"Can you light me one?" Johnny took one of his fabrications and placed it between his lips. VanderHaar gave him the matches, and Johnny carefully struck one into a flame, holding it toward the end of his cigarette, and sucking in the smoke. He handed it to VanderHaar, who took a long and deep drag.

"Not bad, not bad at all, Johnny. You learn fast."

Johnny was proud of his newly learned skill. He lit one for himself and together they were smoking along, as they drove the almost-empty back roads to a yet unknown destination.

"We have to go to Deventer. There is a boat on the IJssel River with lots of Jewish children. They all came from the north of Holland. Apparently people from the Resistance smuggled the children out of the City Theater in Amsterdam. They are holding many Jews in prison there, waiting to transport them to Germany. They keep the children separate. The Resistance has been able to free lots of children of all ages. The people in the North have been brave and generous to take the kids into hiding, but there are too many now. We have to check out this boat, see how many they have, and find homes for them."

Johnny remembered his dream from last night, "Do what you have to do, don't worry, trust." He could almost hear Swan's soft whispering voice in his head.

"Let's do it," he said confidently to VanderHaar.

"We're partners now," VanderHaar encouraged him. "I know I can count on you. This is a big mission; we have to find homes for each kid. Most people we know we can trust are already hiding Jews."

Johnny looked to his mentor. For a moment he was tempted to share his dream but instead he shared the questions that had kept his mind busy for a long time.

"How can people be so cruel? There is absolutely no reason to hurt these children."

He didn't expect an answer but wanted to express his astonishment about the absolutely ridiculous way the Germans were treating the Jews, about the unnecessary chaos all of life was in, which seemed only to get worse.

VanderHaar listened and let Johnny vent his feelings.

"What is the purpose of life, if so many people are being killed for no reason?" Johnny lit one of his self-rolled cigarettes and started puffing as hard as he could.

"What is the purpose of your life, VanderHaar?"

VanderHaar let down his guard, as he too lit up one of the cigarettes. The car soon filled with a waft of smoke. Johnny rolled down the window to get some fresh air.

"I suppose it is love, Johnny. I love my wife and my two daughters."

"Yet you risk your life and perhaps even their lives."

"True, like so many others do."

"Do you believe in God?"

"I think God must be a force of love."

They entered the city of Deventer as they continued their conversation.

"So, you'd rather die for love than witness the injustice?"

"You're right, and I believe Angela, my wife, feels the same way. For her own safety, she doesn't know my whereabouts, but she believes in me and supports everything I do. That is love, that is God."

Johnny was silent for a moment, as he thought of his own parents, of Mara, Joop, and of the farm families. Everyone was risking their life for what they believed to be right. He was satisfied with his conclusion and grateful for this conversation.

"So, the purpose of life is love—to serve love, no matter what."

Once again, he thought of Swan's words: do what you have to do; trust.

They reached the river and turned further south. The streaming water of the IJssel was flowing steadily and elegantly up north toward the Zuiderzee.

"You can't stop a river from flowing," VanderHaar concluded their conversation.

As the city became more distant, VanderHaar pulled his car over. He pointed at a boat about five hundred yards from the car.

"That must be the boat. It fits the description—a blue gate. It is the only boat with a blue gate."

"Let's go together."

They each opened the car door to either side and simultaneously stepped out of the car.

"What's the code?" Johnny asked.

"Nice weather today, not so?"

They took in the fresh air, passing some of the boats, listening to the sound of the cobbling waves breaking softly at the riverbank.

Everything seemed calm. They stood in front of what looked like a houseboat, painted blue and white, with small windows, too small to reveal what was going on inside. The blue gate opened to a tiny improvised garden with a few geraniums, still blooming despite the cold early fall weather. Beautiful red-and-white flowers adorned the front of the boat.

They carefully stepped onto the wooden deck and knocked on the door.

A young woman with two long, brown braids on either side unlocked the door and peeked through it.

"Nice weather today, not so?"

She smiled and welcomed them into a small room with eight cribs carefully spaced next to each other on either side. In the back were a couch, a table, and two chairs. Very simple, but practical.

"Quiet; they are sleeping right now. The nurse just left. Many of the kids are sick, but this little boy just came last night. Can you take him? We don't want him to become sick."

Johnny looked at the boy in the crib. His eyes were closed.

"Can I hold him?" Johnny asked.

The woman bent over to gently take him out of his crib. He was wrapped in a soft blanket. She handed him to Johnny. *Do what you have to do, trust...*

The baby opened his eyes and big, brown eyes looked straight at Johnny.

Johnny awkwardly stroked his cheek while supporting his head with his other arm.

VanderHaar saw the connection and immediately suggested the baby could come to the headmaster's family, Johnny's parents. The mother was dark. The baby could pass for her grandson from Amsterdam.

"We have to ask first; we'll be back soon."

Johnny handed the baby back to the woman with the long brown braids. They exchanged a warm smile.

"Take good care of him. I'll see you soon," as though Johnny already knew that this little being would become part of his family.

They walked back to the car and without any interruptions, they made it to the headmaster's house. Mother was home, wondering what VanderHaar and Johnny needed.

"Mom, a baby, we can take him in."

"He can be your grandson from Amsterdam, who is sick and needs some extra care."

"We have to talk to your dad first. It is dangerous with the Germans next door," she said.

"They'll never notice. We can get the papers organized," said VanderHaar.

"Yes, Mom, he could easily be part of the family. You have dark hair, and so does Joop. They won't know."

Dad walked in and heard what was going on.

It didn't take long for him to agree.

"This may be a leap of faith, but we have to trust that this is the right thing to do. Bring the baby home. We have a crib upstairs and we'll get what we need to take care of the boy."

Johnny hugged his parents.

"Thanks so much. We'll be back in a few hours."

VanderHaar too was grateful and relieved. They left the house and jumped in the car.

By now it was mid-afternoon. They drove the same back roads, smoked some more of Johnny's self-rolled cigarettes, and before they knew it, they were driving along the same river they enjoyed earlier that day, except now the water reflected an almost orange hue from the late afternoon sun. Birds were circling over the water, and a long workboat was softly stuttering up stream. A moment of peace. You would never know a war was going on. You would never know that in less than a mile on a friendly blue-and-white boat with flowering geraniums more than eight babies were kept hidden from the enemy, a young woman with two long, dark braids was taking a chance to save these eight lives, and who knows how many young lives she had saved before.

They stopped the car at the same spot as before, entered the deck, and knocked on the door.

"Nice weather today, not so?"

The door opened. The woman handed him the boy.

"Take the blanket; he came like this. We also know his name. It is Robbie. Here, you can see it embroidered in the blanket."

Johnny could not believe his eyes.

"Robbie—my baby nephew in Amsterdam, his name is also Robbie."

In a flash, he saw Swan's face and heard her saying, Trust, do what you have to do. She was right. This was so perfect. We can just pretend this little baby is my nephew.

"We have to go now," VanderHaar urged him to get ready to go.

"Come back for the other children," the woman with the long braids said. "We also need clothing and food. It is getting cold outside."

VanderHaar let her know that he would be back that same week and provide her with what she needed.

They quickly said goodbye and drove off, back to their little village, where the headmaster and his wife wholeheartedly embraced their new child.

VanderHaar quickly left, and Johnny was happy to enjoy his mother's leftover food from dinner that night.

But not for long.

HIDING

That same evening Mara came home late. Johnny detected a distressed look on her otherwise serene and calm face. She was waiting for a moment alone with Johnny.

"VanderHaar is in jail. Betrayal. You must hide right now."

"Where will I go?"

"Dora is waiting for you. Go to the farm."

"What about Robbie?"

"They don't know about Robbie; he is probably safe."

"How could all this happen so fast?"

"No questions, Johnny, go now. I'll come later this week with an update."

*　　*　　*

"Mom, Dad, I am leaving, I must go right now. Please take good care of Robbie. I'll be with Dora, and I'll be back when it is safe again. Give me Jerry's books."

"How are you going? You don't have a bike, and it's dark outside."

"I'll walk. Once I am on the moors, it'll be deserted. If they come looking for me, you have no idea where I am."

"Of course."

"I'll be back when everything is safe."

Mara urged Johnny to leave now, before it was too late.

Johnny left.

*   *   *

His plan was to go to Dora. She would definitely know a place where he could stay. Jerry would be happy to be able to read again. His backpack was heavily loaded with books on law.

"What good is law, if nobody follows the law? Who makes the laws anyway? If there is something like a natural law, how could all this be possible?" Johnny's mind continued to ponder.

"Didn't VanderHaar say the purpose of life is love, to serve love, no matter what." As Johnny was pondering these words, he decided that no unjust law could destroy love; that it would survive even death. No one could take love from you; never. Not the Nazis, nobody.

Johnny was furious inside that the Nazis had captured his best friend and mentor. "Who could have betrayed them?" he wondered. "Was the woman on the boat safe? And what about the children? Or maybe it had nothing to do with their trip, maybe VanderHaar was betrayed on a different mission."

He wouldn't know until Mara could come and see him.

*   *   *

It was cold outside. Cold and dark. Johnny walked fast through the desolate streets. The small houses were slightly lit behind the closed curtains. Who knows what whispering voices were saying behind those curtains? Who knows what fear was felt behind those curtains? Who knows what treacherous plans were concocted behind those curtains? It was clear to Johnny that silence was the most important defense. One word and many lives could be in danger.

Johnny kept walking faster and faster. He knew the road so well, but mostly he biked this route, and walking through the night with an ever heavier weighing backpack filled with Jerry's law-books seemed to make this trip endless. He finally reached the outskirts of the village. He was no longer supported by the light of the occasional street lantern and by the dim light coming from behind the curtains in each little house.

He reached the moor, the open sky, and millions of stars. He knew no one would come here at this hour. He felt safe and free. He remembered the hand-rolled cigarettes, still crunched up in his pocket. He took one, and struck a match to light it.

It tasted good. He enjoyed the smell and tried to blow circles from his mouth, as he had seen his father do. The cigarette gave him the feeling that VanderHaar was still with him. He felt strong. Nothing could stop him. He enjoyed the final part of his trip, and when he finally reached Dora's farm, it was pitch black. Everyone must be sleeping. Not wanting to wake anyone, Johnny made his way to the barn. Both his body and mind felt exhausted. He knew where the hay was and climbed the ladder to the loft, where he finally let go of his backpack. He improvised making his own bed in the hay and covered himself with a blanket of the prickly dried grass. He was too tired to worry about anything. He knew the morning light would wake him up, and once he smelled the coffee, he would go into the kitchen after first blowing his bird whistle. His eyelids became heavy and before long he drifted off into a deep dreamless sleep.

"What are you doing here?"

It was the voice of Jerry that woke him up.

"Hi Jerry, how do you like your new home? I thought I'd visit you and bring you your books."

Jerry stared at his brother with a look of disbelief, but he didn't want to ask what really brought Johnny to the farm.

"Does Dora know?"

"She knows I'm coming, but it was late last night. I didn't want to wake anyone up."

"Well, let's go and have your favorite breakfast then."

Johnny blew his familiar bird whistle to let Dora know he was here. Jerry grabbed the bags with the books and hid them under the hay off in a corner.

"Thanks, Johnny, for bringing these. I was getting terribly bored up here and thought I might have to help in the field or with the cows. These books will certainly take care of it."

Johnny smiled. He was glad to see his brother in good spirits and for a moment, he forgot all about what had happened the day before.

Together they entered the kitchen. Aromas of fresh morning coffee, fried sizzling bacon, and freshly baked bread welcomed them. Three other young men were already at the table. Dora wiped her hands on her apron and came over to hug Johnny.

"I'm so glad you made it safe."

More young men entered the kitchen. There were eleven of them in total. They could barely fit around the large kitchen table and had to rearrange their plates to make sure there was room. Johnny was immediately taken by their poise and focus, as they introduced themselves to him. Nikko seemed to be their leader. He had a stern look, but when he smiled, Johnny could see that a wonderful person was hiding behind his intense expression. The conversation was light, mainly discussing the delicious foods offered to them by Dora. Nikko seemed to be checking him out. For a minute he felt uncomfortable. What does he want from me?

Dora was entertaining them all with her light sense of humor. "How are the sheep, guys?" she teased, knowing that none of them actually worked with the sheep. Or, "Did you manage to milk Reina the cow?" The guys were playing along. It was a little confusing for Johnny, but he would soon find out who the farm workers really were.

After breakfast, all the men left, except for Nikko. He lingered till even Jerry left the kitchen to get his work done, then he got up and moved to the other side of the table, taking a seat right next to Johnny's.

THE INVITATION

Dora was cleaning up the breakfast table. She poured some of the left-over coffee in both Johnny's and Nikko's cups.

"I have the feeling you two need some private time," she accurately sensed, and left the kitchen to the two young men.

Johnny was surprised to be sitting here in Dora's familiar kitchen, alone with Nikko, a man whom he had met less than an hour ago, and for whom he felt great respect for no apparent reason.

Nikko bent over to Johnny and spoke in an almost whispering voice about the unfairness of the war and about his feelings of wanting to do something about it. Johnny recognized just about everything Nikko was saying, as he remembered the missions he had undertaken with VanderHaar.

"Johnny—or may I call you Buter?" Nikko said with a smile on his face.

How did Nikko know his name Buter? He must know VanderHaar.

"Have you heard from VanderHaar? How do you know my name?"

Nikko's facial expression changed as he spoke about VanderHaar.

"Mara didn't tell you?"

"She did. She said VanderHaar is in jail."

Nikko took a sip from his coffee. There was a moment of silence. It seemed he was searching for words. Finally, he spoke without trying to make it less painful, telling Johnny the plain truth.

"He is dead, Johnny. They shot him, the beasts. They shot him."

Johnny remained motionless at this news. His friend VanderHaar had been shot. He risked his life to save others. Now he was dead. He inspired Johnny to do the same, and right then and there, Johnny felt he had to make a choice. Would he let his life be ruled by fear, or would he too risk his life for the truth?

Nikko gave Johnny the time to sit with his reaction. He waited for him to speak. When their eyes finally met, Johnny recognized that same strength which he had admired in VanderHaar.

"Did you know him well?" Johnny asked.

"We worked together for the last few years in the Resistance. VanderHaar was brilliant, and his network was strong and sound, until recently. We still don't know who the betrayer is, therefore we have to be extremely careful. He told me about you, and about your courage. I am honored to meet you, Johnny."

Johnny became shy at these words. He never thought of himself as courageous. He just did what he had to do. He thought of his parents, who were now hiding the Jewish boy, Robbie, while the Germans were occupying the school next door. That was courageous.

His parents couldn't hide. They were exposed to the eyes of the German soldiers.

"Johnny, we need your help."

"How can I help?"

"You can join our team. We are the so-called farm workers. We live in a hole under the ground. We communicate with the British and pass on important messages."

Johnny listened attentively as Nikko continued.

"The English drop weapons, and we distribute them."

Johnny asked in disbelief, "You do all this under the smoke of Camp Erika?"

"That's right. It is the safest place. No one would expect this to happen in the den of the lion, would they? And Dora feeds us all," Nikko explained, and then paused, giving Johnny the opportunity to make up his mind. Finally, he asked, "What do you think? You want to be part of our group?"

Johnny knew that this was his opportunity to make a serious contribution to help end the war. After all the injustice he had witnessed, it was not hard for him to make that decision.

"I will be honored to join your group," he replied. A sense of strength filled him, like he had never experienced before. He knew that from now on, he had to let go of all his attachments to family and friends, and focus on what he strongly believed in, and he knew that his loved ones would support him in doing so.

Now that VanderHaar was no longer alive, he had to step into his shoes, knowing that his life too might be in danger. Nonetheless he agreed to go with Nikko and was eager to see the hole under the ground, which would become his home for months to come. He finished his coffee and got up.

"Show me," he said to Nikko. "Introduce me to my new friends."

Nikko slapped him on the shoulder.

"Great work, Buter," he smiled. "From now on that's what we'll call you, and we've got to get you some false identity papers. I'll work on that."

Dora entered the kitchen. She didn't need an explanation. She smiled at both young men.

"Let me know if you need anything."

Johnny and Nikko walked out the door. The morning sun shed its glow over the moors ahead of them. They kept walking an invisible path. Nikko knew where he was going. Johnny was curious about where his new team would be hiding.

They walked for about a mile. There was hardly any open space now. They made their way through the bushes.

"Look!" Nikko showed Johnny a dark green bush full of leaves. He moved the leaves aside, and there was a small gas stove. "Sometimes we do our cooking here."

Johnny looked at him in disbelief.

"What if they find you?"

Nikko smiled. "Don't worry, we always have people out watching. As soon as anything looks suspicious, the bird whistle gets passed on. You better get your whistle down soon."

Johnny immediately joined his thumb against the tip of his index finger, creating a circle, and brought it to his mouth, blowing out the purest bird whistle. He clearly impressed Nikko, because Nikko started looking for the bird. Johnny burst out in laughter. He showed Nikko his trick.

"Well done," Nikko said. "That whistle will come in handy. Make sure the guys know."

Johnny looked around. There was nothing that gave away a hole in the ground with a group of guys living in it. The moor was peaceful and quiet, with no one to be seen. They walked on for about a hundred yards. There was a slight hill. Nikko walked up to the hill and uncovered some greens, under which the handle became visible.

"Come quickly, now we have to move fast. Going in and out is risky."

Johnny moved forward as Nikko opened the hatch. A sturdy ladder took him down. Nikko followed him. They entered the hole. Johnny could not believe his eyes. A perfect cozy living space was cleverly designed. The walls were covered with parachute material. Some guys were playing chess, and someone else was reading. Nikko introduced Johnny.

"Guys, this is Buter; he is one of us."

Johnny recognized some of the faces from the breakfast table at Dora's. They smiled at him, and each one introduced himself.

"Make yourself comfortable, Buter," one of the guys offered. "You want to play a game of chess?"

Johnny agreed to the game and before long, he had made a friend and felt at ease with the rest of the crew in his new "home."

AMSTERDAM—HUNGER

Tulip bulbs and onions—the only food that was available in Amsterdam. The war had raged on, at least in the northern part of the Netherlands. The Germans had cut off all transportation to the west of Holland as a contra-measure to the train strike organized by the English during their successful attempt to beat the Germans in Arnhem. For six long weeks, during the immense cold weather, the Germans blocked all transportation to the west. No food was able to come in.

Henk was still teaching at the school, making a salary, but even with money there was not much to buy. Edith and Mark were retreating more and more into their room. They had made it so far through the war. No one ever discovered the hiding place of Edith and Mark. Life was tense at times, but in the end, they learned to live together. Edith had given up hope. She never heard from Truus; she never heard from Dr. Polak; she and Mark carried their grief inside.

Robbie was a happy kid. He started to walk and talk. At first Edith was Antie, and Mark was Unkie, but before long he could say Aunt and Uncle. He was a smart little kid. In a way, it was good that he was raised by four adults, because once he started walking, his curiosity was unstoppable. He often went on his scientific explorations, not knowing the safety rules yet, and he desperately needed to be supervised by someone who could prevent a major calamity.

They all loved him. His innocent yet inquiring big brown eyes were full of life and could make everyone forget, even just for a moment, what was going on outside.

*   *   *

There was hardly any food left in the city. For many days, Agnes waited in line for hours, only to come home with some watery potatoes or soup made from potato peels. People were starving to death. Henk had been teaching all through the war. The stories he brought home were no longer the uplifting stories of his students that kept his passion for life going. Children stopped coming, some were very sick, and some had died of hunger. The war was striking everyone.

One day it became too much. Agnes couldn't bear it any longer. She knew that this hunger was mainly in the west, and that Henk's family in the east of Holland would probably be able to help out. The question was how to get there.

"The only way to do it is to go by bike," Agnes brought up at the dinner table.

"I won't let you go on that old piece of rust without rubber tires," Henk objected. "Besides, we're in the dead of winter. This will cost you your life. I don't want you to go."

"Jenny, our neighbor went, and she did well. I can do this."

Mark too thought this trip was way too dangerous to undertake. But Agnes kept insisting, and her determination convinced the others that they had no choice but to let her go.

Agnes was worried for Robbie. She was no longer able to feed him. She noticed his bones showing through his skin.

"The only solution is to go to your parents, Henk." Agnes spoke with fortitude. "They will have plenty of food."

Agnes had already taken the bike from the small shed in their tiny backyard. It was rusted but still had a working light. The pedals were in good shape and so was the saddle. The rubber on the tires was gone. There was no way around it. They had to turn in the rubber a long time ago. The Germans wanted it, and there had been no need to hold on to it because nobody thought they would need this bike any time soon. Rather than making themselves suspicious, they handed in the rubber, leaving the metal tires bare.

"It can be done," Agnes said with confidence. "Jenny did it, and she stayed overnight with some farm families. She had to pay, mind you; some of these people are trying to get rich off us, but nonetheless, she did it. They have food."

No one argued with Agnes. They admired her courage and determination. Henk drew her a map, explaining clearly which roads to take. She dressed warm. Layer upon layer, to keep the heat in.

"Biking will keep me warm," she said, but everyone knew it was brutal out there, and she needed every precaution to prevent getting frostbite. She left with warm hugs and words of encouragement to send her off.

There was a lot of traffic on the streets. She passed the community kitchen, where she had been able to get food, if you could call it that, in exchange for the food stamps they now received weekly. She would come home with watery potato peel soup, or a sugar cane, but never enough to feed five hungry stomachs.

Thinking of Robbie growing thinner and thinner gave her the courage to keep biking through the cold of winter. If she kept up this pace, she might be able to get there by the evening. She dreaded the thought of having to stay overnight at a farm with strangers. The farmers along the way were making good money, asking ridiculous prices for the slightest amount of food. Luckily, she didn't have to do this. Henk's parents would have plenty of food to share. She was looking forward to seeing them. It had been a long time since they spoke. The war had kept them apart.

*   *   *

It didn't take long before she had found a steady rhythm, keeping a momentum going, which was fine for a while. The movement of her body generated enough heat to keep her warm, almost sweaty at times. There were more bikers on the road. She focused on the person in front of her and tried to keep up. It made it easier that way. She had no idea who this stranger was but for sure someone with the same courage, like all the other people going east to get food. After the initial fatigue, she just kept going, almost automatically. She hardly noticed the sun dropping lower in the sky, almost ready to rest its golden face on the white bed of snow. The woman in front of her stopped and turned into a driveway, entering a farm. Agnes was alone now.

She began to feel how tired she was. Maybe she should take a rest. She could; she had some money to pay for an overnight. The evening was approaching. She had lost all sense of distance. Maybe she could ask at one of those farms. She slowed down. She had been very lucky. The wind was at her back for almost the entire time. Now the wind was picking up. Light snowflakes were falling from the sky, as darkness began to set in. Agnes made the decision. She turned her wheel and drove into an uneven bumpy driveway. She placed her bicycle against the shed and knocked on the door.

"Excuse me, are you taking bikers going east?" she said sounding more confident than she felt. "I just need a bed for the night; I'll be leaving early in the morning."

The man at the door looked at her with great empathy.

"I don't usually," he said, "but I'm sure my wife will be fine having you over for the night. You must be hungry. We don't have much either, but at least we are eating real food."

Before long, Agnes found herself in front of a wood stove, with a bowl of hot soup, three children curiously checking her out, and a wonderful couple who did everything to make her comfortable. She was lucky. She almost felt guilty that she was enjoying this delicious soup. She soon warmed up. She could feel the hot liquid warming her from the inside. Her body relaxed, and she was ready to answer the questions fired at her by three curious children—a girl of about seven with two long, blond braids and big blue eyes, and two boys looking close in age, about three or four years old. Both boys had blond hair, and only one of them had blue eyes. The girl started out, first hesitantly but soon comfortably, because Agnes was happy to tell about her adventure. For a moment, she forgot her own world, her own worries, and found herself absorbed in the innocence of the children.

"How far did you ride your bike?"

"Was it cold?"

"Where did you come from?"

"Do you like chocolate?"

"Do you want to see our book?"

"You want to read us a story?"

Agnes was overwhelmed by their bubbling questions and tried to answer them one at the time. Yes, she loved chocolate, she just couldn't remember the last time she had had any chocolate. And yes, she'd love to read them a story, as they handed her an almost antique version of the fairytale book from Anderson. Soon she was enwrapped in the story of Snow White and the seven dwarves, with three kids curling up against her on the couch. She thought of her Robbie. It won't be long before he too will ask her to read stories. She thought of his meager body, of the sparse food they had been living off these past few months. She promised him she would come back with delicious food. He would miss her right now, but she was sure that Henk, Edith, and Mark would take extra good care of him. She was surprised that she was able to let her mind trail off while she was reading Snow White. The children were enjoying the story.

Then her eye caught something that startled her. One of the boys, his head so close to hers as she was reading the story—his hair, yes, it was blond, but at the roots there was an ever so slight sign of dark hair showing. It all came together. Her hosts, who never even shared their names—of course they didn't take in people. They were hiding this little boy who looked like one of theirs, and only up close could you see that his hair was dyed. His eyes were dark, but so were the eyes of the father. The woman was blond and fair. It could be a perfect family if you didn't know. She realized they took a great risk by taking her in. Just like she and Henk almost never had visitors, making sure no one knew about Mark and Edith.

The story ended. The kids went to bed, and her hosts thanked her for being so nice to the children.

"They don't see many people around these days."

Agnes understood why and decided not to let them know she knew. That would only cause anxiety. She felt honored that they had trusted her, taking her in for the night.

"You must be tired now; why don't you go to sleep? Your bed is made. We'll get you breakfast in the morning, so you are rested and well-fed for another long day on the road."

Agnes was grateful and before long she was sound asleep. It was still dark when she woke up. She had no idea what time it was. Her body ached from the overuse of her muscles. She heard talking. Her host must not be aware how thin the walls were, and how easy the sound traveled. She couldn't help but listen. It sounded like an argument.

"You were stupid to let her so close to the children. What if she noticed?"

"Well, you are the one who let her in. She seemed trustworthy, I agree. I was happy for the kids to have a new and friendly person over. Their world is becoming so small. All they feel is fear, I wanted them to have a different experience."

Agnes could hear them word for word. Should she tell them not to worry? Should she tell them about Edith and Mark? Should she tell them that she understood their feelings? That she knew what it was to live in fear every day, wondering whether someone had become suspicious, betraying them for selfish or hateful reasons? She couldn't. The only thing she could do was to make them believe that she didn't know what she had seen. The voices went on, and Agnes gave up trying to hear what they were saying. She stretched out her legs to ease the stiffness and focused on her breath, hoping for sleep to take over.

This time, it was the smell of fresh coffee that woke her up. It was still dark. She switched on her light and saw that it was only six in the morning. She heard the children's voices. If she would get up now, she could be on the road by seven. That would allow her to arrive in Vroomshoop in the early afternoon. She got up, not without pain. She worked through it as she packed her few belongings and made her bed.

Ready for the journey, she walked down the stairs. She purposely stepped down with a little more force than she would otherwise, to let the family know that she was coming. Not without results, because all three children came running to her.

"Will you tell us another story?"

Their mother came after them. "Not now. Agnes has to travel a long way today. She has to leave right after breakfast."

She warmly invited Agnes into the kitchen. The table was set for her with a delicious breakfast. They even had real butter. She looked at her host with gratitude. She wanted to tell her not to worry. But if she did, she would only cause more anxiety.

"Did you sleep?"

Agnes nodded; she made a joke about her stiff muscles. The children had already made drawings of the story she had told the night before.

"For you, for you, take it."

She looked at each of them and smiled. She folded them ever so carefully and slid them in a side pocket of her bag.

"Thank you so much." She gave each of them a big hug. She made it a point not to look at the little boy's hair. Instead she smiled at her hostess, who visibly relaxed.

They waved her out as she mounted her bike.

"Will you come back?" the children asked.

"I would love to," she answered, but her hosts didn't say anything. She understood why.

"Ride safely!" were the only words they called after her as she turned out of the driveway. The sun had just risen, and it was light enough to see where she was going. Luckily there was not much snow. It was cold though. She set her mind to her goal, and her legs followed, pushing the pedals in her now-familiar rhythm.

FISHING AND OTHER DANGERS

Johnny knew that chess was not the only thing the guys played in this self-made hole under the ground. That same evening, he was initiated into the life of the Resistance, as they were planning their next move to undermine the work of the Germans. They all hovered around a small radio through which they were in contact with the English. The English were dropping weapons, medicine, food, and even cigarettes. Before a dropping, there was a special code: "Ducks are quacking in the pond." That meant that there were no obstructions. Everything was safe. Right there on the land, less than half a mile from the internment camp, the most dangerous missions against the Nazis were carried out. Nobody expected this to happen; that's why it was safer than any other place.

The next day everyone made their preparations. Nikko instructed the guys on where to take the weapons. Johnny had no idea that Dora was so deeply involved as well. Not only was she hiding people, she was also hiding the weapons that were sent by the British, and found a safe temporary home under her hay in the barn, where he had spent the night not too long ago. The droppings would happen around eleven at night.

During the next day they took turns listening to the radio. The code was still on. "Ducks are quacking in the pond." They all went to Dora's farm to "work" as farm workers, but more so to get a taste of her delicious cooking. They were talking fish. Dora brought up that none of them had caught any fish lately. She had the fishing poles ready and asked if they wanted to catch some, so she could cook them for dinner.

"We are so many now," Nikko said. "You know how long it takes before we catch a fish?"

Dora was laughing. "True, true, you guys have different things to do. No more time to go fishing."

Johnny loved to fish. He had gone fishing in that stream even before the war. He loved sitting by the water, just waiting till he could feel the slightest tug on the fishing pole, bringing in a fish. He was always proud to bring some home. One day, he even caught five fish of reasonable size. The whole family enjoyed fried fish, and Johnny was beaming that night. It had been a while ago.

"I'll take the pole and will bring you some fish soon," he promised.

*   *   *

They took turns walking back to the hiding hole. It was quiet as ever on the moors. That evening they made themselves ready. They changed into their camouflage clothing. It was dark. An almost-new moon shed the slightest light and other than the stars, there was no other light. They climbed out of the hole one by one and spread themselves out strategically. It was cold, but luckily there was no snow.

Johnny found himself under a bush, waiting for the sound of the small plane that would be flying over very soon. He looked around. There were twelve of them hiding. Here and there, he saw the dark shadow of one of his mates, slightly moving, but only if you knew they were there could you distinguish the men from the bushes. There was an open field. That's where the weapons would fall. The utter silence was palpable. Time seemed to pass very slowly. Or was it that he lost all sense of time? What seemed an eternity may have been just a few minutes. He knew what to do. As soon as the plane came over and dropped the guns, they would run and collect them, and return to their hiding place. Wait for the plane to be gone, and one by one they would go back to their hole.

In the distance, he heard the soft buzz of what could be the plane. He listened intently as the sound drew closer. His heart began beating faster. A big black bird was making its way toward him. Almost immediately there was an enormous sound and lots of weapons falling out of the sky. They weren't quite falling straight down. Small parachutes allowed them to veer through the air before hitting the ground. It all went very fast. Before he knew it, the plane had taken off as fast as it came. He ran over to where he could see the guns on the frozen earth. He took them and hid back under the bush. He noticed his friends doing the exact same thing. When everything was quiet again, they returned to the hole, relieved that this mission had succeeded. They did a count, and they got them all.

"We're not done yet," Nikko said. "We have to take turns taking the weapons to Dora's farm. We can't wait till tomorrow."

"What are the weapons used for?" Johnny asked Nikko.

"You don't want to know. Just in case they round us up."

Johnny was used to not knowing. He didn't ask. He changed out of his camouflage clothes into some other warm clothes and crawled into his sleeping bag. He was thinking up a plan to get Dora some fish, as he had promised. Half awake, half sleeping, he came up with a luminous plan. He needed to speak to Mara though. She could help him.

Mara stopped by the next day. She came to let everyone know that the weapons were already picked up, and safely brought to their destination. Johnny sought out a chance to take his sister aside.

"Mara, can you bring me a hand grenade?"

"Why, what are you planning to do?"

"Don't worry, I'll put it to good use. I'll go fishing."

Mara looked puzzled, "Fishing with a hand grenade?"

Johnny saw he needed to explain, in order for his sister to fulfill his request. "I'll throw it in the river, it will explode at the bottom, and the fish will come to the surface. Lots of fish will come to the surface. I also need a net; can you get that for me?" He told her that he promised Dora that he would bring enough fish to feed everyone. Mara thought the plan was rather clever and agreed that she would see what she could do.

"Before you leave, how is Robbie? Is he adjusting to his new home?"

Mara's face lit up in a smile. "Everyone is fond of him; he is a happy little guy. Mom and Anna are spoiling him. Anna acts like she is his mother. You should see the two of them. Robbie loves her too. "

"And the Germans?"

"No problem. Only Franz and Albert come around almost every day, but they are friendly. Mother has knitted them some warm underwear, because they were freezing in those stupid uniforms. I don't think they are bad guys. Of course we cannot take a risk, but so far everything is fine."

"What about the other Germans?"

"They basically do their own thing. They hardly come into the house. If they do, it is only to get some food or some ingredient they need for their own cooking. But Joop goes there every night. He plays chess, and in the meantime, he listens in on their conversations. If he catches anything that sounds suspicious, he can pass that on right away. He pretends not to understand or speak any German. But he is a good chess player, and they like that."

Johnny was proud of his brother Joop. He had never thought that all the evenings he taught his brother chess would come in handy during this time of danger.

"Thanks, Mara, for all you do. You are an inspiration."

"So are you, bud, or shall I call you... Buter?" she laughed.

"Take care, sis."

Johnny made his way back into the hut as Mara jumped on her bike crossing the moors, heading back home.

THE OTHER ROBBIE

The landscape started to become familiar. Agnes had been biking steadily keeping herself warm and motivated by the thought of Robbie taken care off. She experienced a strength she was not aware she had. Luckily the snowfall did not make it past a few dwindling snowflakes occasionally decorating the sky. In the distance, she saw the contour of the village. It seemed like all her fatigue fell off of her, and she was charged with renewed strength.

Her heart leapt up as she came closer to the village. She would be there in just a few more minutes. She was looking forward to seeing her in-law family, and she was wondering how the war was affecting them. It was late afternoon. The sun was making its way down already. School would be out, and Father would be home as well. She entered the familiar street and stopped in front of the house right by the school. She opened the gate and rested her bike against the fence. Luckily, Mother saw her and came out to greet her. She walked all the way to the bike. She hugged her long, and during that hug, a quick conversation took place.

"We are hiding a Jewish boy. His name is Robbie; we tell them it is your son, our grandson. Germans are in the school and in the house. Play along. Please."

This is not what Agnes had expected, but she quickly agreed. They walked in.

"Robbie," she said, and walked up to the little boy, who indeed looked just like her own Robbie. She picked him up and kissed him.

"Don't you look good! Ma and Pa are taking good care of you."

Anna stepped forward. "I'm his main caretaker," she said proudly.

Mother laughed. "True enough, Anna and Robbie have been inseparable ever since he came.

Mother continued, "Let me introduce Franz and Albert, two German soldiers. They live in the school."

Agnes tried to hide her look of surprise and possible dismay at the sight of the two German boys. They looked young. They greeted her politely. She dared not to ask any questions.

"*Wir lieben das kleine Männchen,*" they told her.

"They love Robbie," Mother quickly translated.

Father walked in and being in the presence of Henk's parents made her feel like a child again, being welcomed, nourished, and cared for. Her worries fell off her shoulder for a short while. Mother gave her delicious food, which she hadn't had for a long time.

*   *   *

At the dinner table, they finally could talk freely. They asked about Henk, Robbie, the war in Amsterdam, the Hunger Winter. They wanted to know everything. Agnes couldn't help herself. She burst into tears. Not many words were needed. Agnes was careful not to tell about Edith and Mark. She also didn't talk about the Jewish boy in the family where she stayed overnight. They let her cry and the warmth of their presence helped Agnes relax and feel at ease.

Mother asked what kind of food she wanted to take and began packing. Fresh milk, cheese, bread, butter, flour, bacon, fruit, and even a piece of chocolate, and more dry goods that would help the family sustain for a while. Agnes would stay the night and decided to ride back again the next day. She rested. She slept in Johnny's room. She dared not ask where Johnny and Jerry were. The German soldiers did not come back. She looked at Robbie, who was playing with Anna. Mara and Joop too came home. The warmth of the family nourished her heart. And Robbie seemed so naturally belonging to the family. She was grateful that in a small way she could contribute to his safety, just by having her own Robbie.

Before drifting into a deep sleep, she looked around the room. Her eyes caught the family photo on the wall. Henk was there with his younger brother Louis. Behind the two boys stood Father and their step-mother, Father's second wife, who quickly had become "Mother" to all of them. Seated in the photo were the young step-brothers and sisters. Henk's brother Louis had emigrated to the United States only a few years ago. Perhaps Louis couldn't handle the pain of losing his mother. Henk was already grown-up, ready to teach, taking after Father. Louis might never really be able to escape his grief, but he definitely escaped the war.

Agnes thought of family, of Robbie, who was separated from his parents, who might never see his own parents ever again, of Mark and Edith, who were cut off from the world, cut off from their relatives, non-existing, except for the small world in her house. She thought of the young boy with the dark roots in his blond hair. Chocolate, I have to stop by and hand them the chocolate. Tomorrow on the way back I will do that. Her eyelids became heavy and she slid into a world of darkness and silence.

FISH

Dora's kitchen had become a hub of happy men, sitting around her table, eating the deliciously prepared fresh fish from the local river.

"When I promise something, I do it. That is my rule number one," Johnny shared with a big grin on his face. The guys were curious, and Dora had never seen that many fresh fish together since she last went to a market, which was a long time ago, before the war, and only sporadically there was a fish stand. Johnny wondered whether he should tell his secret. They would probably not agree with his adventure, but seeing them all devouring their meal, he decided to let them in. Chances are he would not embark on this kind of adventure again anyway. With a slight allure of bravery Johnny began relating his story.

It started with the grenade Mara had brought him just a few days ago; that along with a net and two buckets. They hid them under a bush; in fact, the same bush where the cooking plate was, which was never used anyway. Nobody ever went there, and it was very well hidden. Very early this morning, Johnny knew to leave the hut before the crack of dawn. He got his buckets, the net, and the grenade from under the bush, and walked to the river. He chose his favorite fishing spot and waited for the sun to rise.

"Grenades are good for fishing," he told the men, "not for killing people."

"Don't tell us you..."

"Yes, I threw the grenade in the river. I could see the explosion, waited for a moment, and threw out the nets to catch all the fish that instantly came to the surface, dead or alive. There were more than I could possibly take. I filled the buckets and walked to the farm. The rest of the story Dora can tell you."

"No one saw you?" Nikko asked.

"Not a soul."

They all clapped for him. It truly was a genius idea, dangerous but genius, with a terrific ending. Johnny had to agree that this was a one-time adventure, not to be repeated. They continued to feast on their delicious meal, forgetting about the tension of war, just celebrating a good catch of fish. What was surprising to all of them was that Johnny was able to leave the hut for a prolonged period of time without anyone missing him. That in fact was a lesson for them all. They should all be aware if one of them stepped out for any period of time.

Mara walked in. Everyone was clapping for her.

"Thanks, Mara!"

Mara gave a quick smile, but it was clear she had another reason for her visit. Nikko got up.

"Need to talk in private?"

Mara nodded, and together they walked away. Reality kicked in. All of a sudden, the tensions of war were palpable once again. They waited for Nikko to return. Some helped Dora clean up, some rolled a cigarette, but they couldn't smoke it. Dora would not have it in her kitchen. Johnny's heart was thumping. What could be of such importance for Mara to come in the middle of the day with a message? It had to be serious.

It was serious. Nikko returned with a grim look on his face. Concern and a slight panic in his eyes told Johnny that something was about to happen. Did it have to do with his fishing adventure? Did someone see him after all? Anything wrong at home? Nikko called for Johnny.

"We need to talk, Johnny."

To the guys, he said, "We'll meet you in the hut in about an hour."

Johnny and Nikko found a quiet spot in one of the barns. Not a person around. Jerry was in the fields helping the farmers. Their only witnesses were the pigs. Big lazy pigs, bathing in the mud, occasionally snorting, letting them know they were there.

Nikko looked at Johnny. "This is very serious, Johnny," his voice trembled. "You, out of anyone I know, I can trust."

Johnny felt his boyish bravado from earlier that day make room for true strength. Nikko trusted him with something very serious. He thought back on his moment with VanderHaar in the car, his dream with Swan, and of Mara's courage. Even though his heart was pounding, he told Nikko he would be there to support him.

"There is a spy in our group," Nikko said.

"A spy?" Johnny replied with disbelief. "How do they know?"

"The weapons were found before they reached their destination. Luckily, they had left Dora's farm. Only a few of us knew where they went. That rules out the others."

"It turns out that VanderHaar too was betrayed by one of us. That was just before you came. Whoever it is, the location of our hut has not yet been given away. It must be someone doing it for the money. So, he stretches it; as long as he can make money, he will give information. Our district commander is looking into it. Bart was the last one to join the group. He found us, didn't really explain how, but made a great story for joining us. I bought into it."

Johnny thought of Bart. He had been very kind to him so far. He didn't seem different from the other guys; in fact, he was the one who offered to play a game of chess with Johnny when he first joined the group. But a spy would never give away his true identity.

"Like you said, Nikko, this *is* very serious. What are we to do?"

"For now, you must keep an eye on Bart, and on everyone else."

"What am I to tell them?"

"Play it cool. Let them know we are up for another dropping in the next week or so, food and cigarettes this time. To be delivered to Warehouse #6. Innocent information but perhaps a good bait."

"Keep track of whoever leaves the hut and how long they are gone for. Most of us are in your position—we are already hiding from the Germans. So I can't imagine anyone but Bart would be gone for a prolonged period of time. Since we haven't paid attention, we could have easily missed it, just like we didn't realize your absence this morning, when you went fishing."

"What if it is Bart?"

"We will know soon."

"Then what?" Johnny feared the answer he was about to hear.

"Then we will have to execute," Nikko said matter-of-factly. "We cannot risk the consequences."

Johnny thought of the possible consequences and how many people might end up being killed if this entire network were to be unraveled. The revenge would be immeasurable. The Germans had their own rigid ways of dealing with any push-back. Johnny quivered at the thought of having to kill one of their men because he was a betrayer. He wouldn't let his mind go any further. He left it to Nikko.

"By the way, Johnny, thanks for the fish," Nikko lightened up the conversation.

"You're welcome, it was truly a pleasure." Johnny grinned again at the thought of his early morning adventure. "Not to be repeated, I know, I know," he added mischievously. He loved switching back to the innocence of his youth, but knew that from now on he would have to step into his manhood. Nikko had business to take care of, and Johnny went back to the hut.

The men were curious and wanted to know what the message was about. Johnny told them about the droppings from England in the next week, food and cigarettes this time. Everything would be taken to Warehouse #6. Maybe this food was destined to go to the west of Holland. People are starving to death right now. There simply is no food.

"Maybe we get to keep some real cigarettes," one of the guys said. "I'm tired of rolling my own."

"Maybe." Johnny smiled. He kept a close eye on Bart. His reaction seemed normal, just like the other guys.

THE TRIP BACK

Everyone convinced Agnes to rest another day and regain her strength in preparation of the trip back. Agnes finally agreed. She enjoyed hanging out with Mother, Anna, and Robbie. They even went for a walk. She loved being in the small village. It was so quiet and friendly. If you didn't know, you could barely feel there was a war going on. Of course, reality was right in her face when she saw the Germans occupying Father's school.

"How can you live with them?" she asked.

"We don't, we put up with them."

"What about the two guys in your living room?"

"They are young kids, Agnes, they miss their home. They don't want to be in this war."

"You better be careful," Agnes warned her.

Mother switched to a different subject. She asked about Henk, her stepson, and wanted to know everything about what it had been like in Amsterdam. Agnes again told about the hunger, the long lines at the soup kitchen, the people dying, the women traveling for food. She didn't tell them about Edith and Mark. She could, but the less people knew the better. She too had learned the necessity of absolute silence during these times.

Anna and Robbie were off ahead of them playing a game of catch. Robbie could barely run, and he wobbled after Anna. He was so adorable. His puffy cheeks, his big brown eyes, and his mischievous smile were enough to make you fall in love with him. Yes, he could be their grandson from Amsterdam. She wished her Robbie would soon be healthy and chubby just like this child. The day passed easefully, and together they packed the bags on her bicycle with food, drink, and treats. She tried out her bike. It was definitely a lot harder to drive with all that weight. She was glad she waited another day.

But before she knew it, the time had come to say farewell. The big hugs were enough for her to last another trip. It was very early in the morning. This time she was determined to make the trip in one long day. She made sure the bar of chocolate was within easy reach. She had it wrapped with a big "Thank You" written on it. She wanted to bring it to the family she had stayed with on the way up. Mother sent her off.

"Come back soon!"

"When we run out, for sure. Hopefully this war will be over soon."

Agnes disappeared in the distance. Mother went about her daily business.

*   *   *

Agnes felt a renewed strength. She had come this far; the way back should be possible. She was lucky to have the wind supporting her. Her pedaling became almost effortless. If she kept going like this, she would make it by the evening. In her mind's eye, she could see a dinner table filled with delicious and nutritious food. She could see Henk's eyes light up. She could see Robbie devour the sweet pudding she would make. She could see Edith and Mark feeling so much better. What a feast it would be. But first, she wanted to stop by the family. She'd just ring the bell, hand the chocolate, thank them, and let them know it was for the children. As she was thinking and dreaming, she kept on pedaling. A steady rhythm, filled with hope for the future.

* * *

She approached the house where she stayed just two nights ago. When she reached the shed, she made a turn inside the property. She rested her bike against the wall, took the chocolate, and walked toward the front door. She rang the bell. No one opened. Something was off. She looked through the window and saw people moving. They are home. She rang again. After a while the door slowly opened.

"We can't take you now," the man said.

"I just came by to thank you for your hospitality. The warmth of your family helped me on my trip. I have food now, but I wanted to give this chocolate bar for your children." She looked past him as she was talking. There was the mother and two of the children. An uneasy feeling crept up inside her.

"You knew."

"Yes, but I never mentioned it to anyone."

"I didn't think so, but my wife, she was so suspicious."

"When did it happen?"

"Yesterday. They knew exactly who they were looking for," the man said.

"We are lucky to still be here. They could have taken us as well. They still might come and take me."

"I am so sorry," Agnes said.

"It's not your fault, but you should go now. We are being watched, and anything suspicious will set off another alarm. They will come back. It is a matter of time. You should go."

Agnes handed him the chocolate.

"For the children, please," she almost begged him to accept her gift, as if she could make it easier for them.

"The best of luck. Have a safe ride home today."

Agnes walked to her bike. Her heart was pounding, and soon she was pedaling with all her might back to Amsterdam. Fear overtook her from time to time. What if the Nazis had discovered Edith and Mark? What was she coming home to? All her dreams from earlier that day were replaced by a wave of fear running through her entire being. She took no time to rest. She kept going without feeling any symptoms of fatigue. "I hope they are safe. They must be safe." These were the only thoughts in her mind.

She finally reached Amsterdam. She biked through the streets. Only a few people were out on the streets. She paid no heed and rode straight to her house. In her backyard, she jumped off. Henk came out immediately, half expecting her, half worried that something might have happened along the way. He embraced her and slowly led her inside. Edith and Mark helped getting her bags with the food.

"What happened?" Henk asked upon seeing her distress? "Are you okay?"

Agnes looked at them, and seeing that everyone was home and that nothing had changed helped her relax.

"I was so worried," she said. "I was so worried that you were discovered by the Germans."

"Let's go inside, have some food, and tell us all about your trip."

"Where is Robbie?" Agnes went to his room, and saw him sound asleep. She stroked him over his cheek. "Robbie, you are safe. Come and have some delicious treats." He opened his eyes, and his innocent smile, his reaching out to her, brought her back to her senses.

Not long after, they sat together in the living room, ate some bread, drank tea with milk, and Henk smoked one of the cigarettes Mother had stuffed in there at the last moment. Agnes told her story. She told them about her guest family, the three blond children, the one with dark roots, her suspicion of them hiding a Jewish boy. She told them about her visit home, about the other Robbie, and as she described him, Edith burst into tears. Mark and Edith had kept their secret for so long, but when Agnes described Robbie, Edith suddenly had a spark of hope.

Edith told Agnes and Henk all about their story, about their own Robbie, how he was taken now almost two years ago.

"Why didn't you tell us?" Agnes asked.

"There is so much sorrow already, we didn't want to bring more sorrow to your house."

Agnes was stunned. What pain they both must have had, not knowing where their own son was, and whether he was still alive.

"You think it could be possible that our Robbie is staying with your parents?"

"Did they call him Robbie because they said he was their grandson?"

"Perhaps, there is no way to know."

"There might be a way. Robbie left wrapped in an embroidered blanket that my mother made for him when she was in jail."

"Perhaps that blanket traveled with him?" Agnes wondered.

"In that case, his name was Robbie already, and your parents thought to make up the story of him being their grandson."

"There is only one way to find out." Agnes felt her strength and determination return. After all she had seen in such a short time, she knew she had to go back. She knew that she had to make that same trip one more time. Mother had said to come back.

"Sure, Agnes, all good and well, but first you must rest and get your strength back," said Henk.

"True, but as soon as I'm ready, I will go again."

She hugged Robbie and pressed him close to her heart. She looked at Edith and Mark. She saw hope in their eyes. She thought of the family she stayed with, the little boy who was taken, the sadness and fear these people must have experienced.

"Soon. I'll go very soon," she smiled.

DISCOVERY

There was nothing different this afternoon from any other day. Some of the guys were just passing time, laying down, daydreaming; some were dealing a hand of cards; and Bart was playing chess as usual. The hut had become their second home, and even Johnny had come to love the small space surrounded by parachute lining and sleeping bags laying around randomly. So far no one had taken it upon himself to keep the space neat and organized. Johnny decided to join the group playing cards. He chose a spot not too far from the entrance to the hut, so he couldn't miss anyone leaving. He kept a peripheral eye on Bart. He could barely believe that he would betray their group.

The rest of the afternoon passed quietly as usual. Nikko came back. He had become quite adept, as did everyone else, at entering the hut with a quick silent movement, closing the trap above his head, while twisting his body and stepping down the ropes. He made almost no sound, which alerted Johnny that it was quite easy to enter and to leave in the dark, without waking up anyone. But Nikko made his arrival known by jumping off, skipping the last few steps on the ladder. Everyone looked up. Nikko held up a bag with sandwiches from Dora's kitchen. The men gathered in a circle and took their evening meal. The thermos with coffee barely had enough coffee for everyone, but small cups were just fine.

"We should be grateful for our food," one of the guys uttered, referring to the immense hunger in the western part of the country.

"Exactly," Nikko agreed," and that is actually the reason I am here." He continued to remind them of the scarcity of food in the western part of the country. "All transportation to that part has been cut off. That's why we have a new mission. Johnny may have told you earlier, and I want to fill you guys in with the details. The droppings will happen in just three days. We all have to pitch in and collect everything, just as we do with the infantry. We stash it under the bushes. The next morning very early, one of the farmers will come by with lots of hay on his wagon. The food goes under the hay, to be taken to the farm, where others will take it to warehouse #6. We expect the food to be there no later than ten in the morning. No one knows about this except for the very few of us involved in the mission."

Johnny was wondering why Nikko provided so much detail. Did he want to make it seem real? What was his tactic here? If the betrayer, whoever it was, wanted, he could turn everyone in by having the Germans come to the dropping. His mind was spinning. Nikko didn't think the suspect would give away their hiding place just yet. He would have done this already. It was clearly about the money. Whoever the spy was, he would communicate the arrival of food at the warehouse. I hope he is right, Johnny thought as he looked around carefully. He studied the faces of each and every one of the guys. His eyes rested on Bart again. He noticed Bart wasn't eating. His sandwich remained untouched in front of him, till one of the guys joked,

"Not eating, Bart? I'll take your sandwich."

But Bart wouldn't have it. He took his sandwich and slid it into his backpack.

"I'll save it for later," he replied. It all seemed normal but not eating was not normal; not for these guys; especially not for Bart.

Nikko excused himself. He left, climbing the rope ladder with the same agility as he came in. This was the usual time for everyone to go out to stretch, walk around, or smoke a cigarette. They took turns. If each of them took no more than five minutes, the break could be done in one hour.

All went according to the usual plan. The guys were discussing Nikko's news. They were excited. It had been a while since the last dropping. It was hard not being able to do anything to help the country. The first night Johnny stayed awake. The few guys who left during the night returned almost within minutes, but Bart didn't leave.

Johnny had to fight the drowsy feeling that arose within him. He could barely keep his eyelids open. They kept falling, and he kept sinking into a state of near sleep.

Suddenly he was alerted. It must have been close to dawn, still pitch black in the hut, but outside the early morning sunlight made it easy for anyone to find their way across the moor. Ever so quietly, a figure moved toward the rope ladder. Though he couldn't see his face, Johnny recognized the slight stoop that belonged to Bart. He watched Bart leave the hut. For a brief second, the morning light entered the dark space. Now it was a matter of staying awake and keeping track of the amount of time Bart would be out. Minutes passed, and no sign of Bart.

In about an hour the guys would wake up. Bart would certainly be back by then. But even then, there was no sign of Bart. The familiar sound of yawning and stretching slowly brought the hut back to life.

Finally, the trap opened. Bart came down, as though he had just stepped out for a few minutes. No one would know, because no one saw him leave about an hour ago. Johnny was clear. Nikko was right. He kept watching Bart. Bart behaved as though nothing had happened.

They all got ready to have breakfast in Dora's kitchen. They left one at the time. Nikko was already at the table, enjoying his steaming hot coffee and his freshly scrambled eggs. When Johnny entered, he did not seek Nikko out. He didn't want to make it obvious he was communicating with Nikko. Surely Bart would be anxious and alert. But Nikko didn't need words to know. When their eyes met, the message was communicated unspoken.

The morning went as usual. Johnny wondered if Dora was aware of what was going on. Perhaps Nikko wanted to spare her this news. She had enough on her plate, feeding them, and hiding several men, including Jerry. Johnny hadn't seen Jerry for a few days now. Dora was able to inform him that Jerry was actually doing some work at the farm, and the remaining time he was studying his law books for when he would go back to school after the war.

When the men had left to go back to their hiding place, Johnny lingered to talk to Nikko.

"What do we do next?"

"I will leave it up to the commander; we need more proof. Keep your eyes open, we have a few days."

Johnny's felt his stomach twist. He knew what was to come, and he was not at ease with it at all.

CONNECTIONS

"Nice weather today, not so?" The kitchen door opened and there was Mara. Johnny's heart skipped a beat. Who told her the code? What did she know about it?

Before he could express his confusion, the woman with the long, dark braids from the boat appeared from behind Mara.

"May I introduce Lisa, my new fellow messenger and friend."

Johnny rose to his feet with utter astonishment. He never expected to see the woman with the long, dark braids again. Lisa greeted him with the same warm smile she had previously on the boat when she handed him Robbie.

"Nice to see you again."

An awkward silence followed their greeting. But Mara had lots to tell. She told him about Robbie, how well he was doing. If he had a chance, he should come home for a visit. Everyone missed him, especially Mother.

Finally, Johnny got himself together and fired one question after another towards Lisa.

"How are the other children on the boat?"

"Who is taking care of them now?"

"How did you find Mara?"

Lisa had no chance to even begin answering his questions. She smiled.

"Hold on, one question at a time."

"The children are fine. VanderHaar had arranged addresses for them all before he was caught."

"The boat is empty now; it was too risky after they found VanderHaar. I decided to leave and join his network here."

"That's how I found Mara. We work together. I have new identity papers and my name is Lisa Smaal."

"I am temporarily staying at your house, so Mara and I can continue our work."

"How was the fish, brother dear?" Mara threw in jokingly.

"Ask Dora; she's the one who cooked them."

"But you are the one who ate them."

"Everyone was happy that day, Mara, thanks to your help."

Dora was quietly witnessing the three youngsters sitting together. She enjoyed their youth, their innocence in the midst of the danger they were exposed to each day. She witnessed the stirrings of new love and smiled, as they continued to chatter and joke.

After some ripples of laughter, they became serious again. Lisa looked at him intensely. She wanted to know about him. He felt an urge to talk about what was going on in his heart. He wanted to tell her about his work with Nikko, about the betrayer, but no words came out. His eyes met Lisa's. He realized, just as this morning with Nikko, no words were needed. She read him, and answered with a warm and compassionate smile. Immediately he felt understood. It gave him courage. He had never felt seen like this. She saw him, she saw who he was, she saw what was going on in him. She met him at a very deep level. His heart filled tangibly with what felt like liquid gold, warmth he had never felt before.

Mara broke the spell.

"We have to go now. No news, just saying hello."

"Come back soon," Dora stepped in, "and be careful, all of you!" A slight tone of deep concern echoed through her voice. "May all this trouble end soon. You are too young to be exposed to all this craziness."

For the first time Johnny saw a different side of Dora. She was always the Big Mama for everyone. Now she looked vulnerable, concerned, and in pain. Her eyes were wet. He gave her a big hug.

"Thanks for all you do, Dora. If it wasn't for you, none of us could do our work."

Dora regained herself and smiled.

"Okay then, stay out of trouble!" She sent them all off with their own missions to fulfill.

THE BLANKET

Whether it was the abundance of food, or the fact that Edith and Mark had entrusted Agnes and Henk with their loss of Robbie, the days following Agnes's return from the east of Holland were light and easeful. Edith even caught herself softly humming a made-up melody to herself. She kept dreaming about Robbie. Would it be possible that he was alive and well? Would such a miracle even exist in the midst of war and destruction? Mark noticed the change in Edith. He too was filled with hope.

"We will know very soon," he reassured Edith, pushing away his own doubts and concerns about what would happen if the child at the headmaster's house turned out to be a nameless child called Robbie just because their grandchild's name was Robbie. He too wanted to believe in the impossible that, even if it was an idle thought, still had brought a spark of light, illuminating their long-kept dark secret. Edith tried to imagine what Robbie would look like. She kept asking Agnes, "Tell me again, what were his eyes like?" "How was his walk?"

Agnes tried as best she could to describe "Robbie."

"He wobbles when he walks. He's so cute, adorable, they love him."

"What else?"

"His eyes are twinkling with a mischievous spark, like he's always up to something." Agnes recalled her memory. "He's a little chubby, but maybe that was just my perception, because everyone here is flesh over bone."

Agnes too did not want to diminish the spark of hope. She never realized how it could infuse life with regained joy. Edith seemed a different person. All Agnes wanted to do was to help her. Her plan to make her second trip soon began to crystallize in her head. It wouldn't be long, she knew. Edith and Agnes had become friends for the first time.

Little Robbie walked in. He had regained his strength. He was rounder, even after just a few weeks of a full stomach at every meal. He too wobbled. His eyes were more curious than mischievous. Robbie was a serious child, growing up amidst adults trying to hide their sorrows from him, pretending happiness. The astute expression in his eyes showed that somehow, he was not entirely unaware of the difficult times. Edith picked him up and held him close to her heart. "Robbie," she whispered softly, "Robbie, Robbie, Robbie." Agnes intensely hoped to uncover the mystery of the hiding place of the child of her guests.

*　　*　　*

"I'm off tomorrow morning," Agnes announced at the breakfast table. "I'm strong enough, the weather has been stable, and I'm sure I can make it in one day this time."

Nobody contradicted her. They were all longing for this trip, hoping for a miracle. The food was getting low as well. She promised Robbie she'd bring back chocolate, and for everyone else lots of fresh creamy cheese, more coffee, and softly baked bread, replacing the stale remains of old bread of her last trip. Henk had checked out her bike, and once again he sent her off with words to be careful, not to stop unnecessarily, but to take rest should she need it.

Agnes made the same trip. It seemed so much easier the second time. Very soon her legs moved automatically, she picked up momentum, and even enjoyed the fresh air blowing through her hair. The city faded into country and the now-familiar roads took her to her destination. It was as if time no longer existed. Her mind became empty with just the steady sound of the pedals of her rusty bicycle. A slight wind in her back supported her on this auspicious trip. She passed the house she had stayed at previously. A voice inside kept urging her to move on, not to stop, not to look, and not to think about the fate of her host family. She had her own mission. She kept going. Darkness fell, but she kept going. She knew the road well now, and nothing could stop her. Late that night she leaned her bicycle against the fence of the headmaster's house. A dim light was burning inside. Someone must still be awake. She knocked on the front door. It slowly opened, and she was welcomed by the surprised look on Mother's face.

"A second trip! You must be exhausted," Mother said. She had Agnes rest in the most comfortable chair in the room. She hurried to the kitchen to make Agnes some hot milk. Agnes was both numb and excited at the same time.

"Mother, before you do anything, tell me about Robbie. What do you know about him? How did he get here?"

Mother came back with a cup of foaming hot milk.

"Here, drink this first, and then we'll talk."

She pushed a stool under Agnes's legs, carefully placing a pillow under her knees. Agnes sipped from the milk. She felt her limbs tingling and her breath easing back to its regular rhythm. Mother pulled a chair up close to her and began lowering her voice.

"Everyone is asleep, let's not wake them up, but we can talk. This is a great time. No Germans around the house, no ears to listen in. But let's whisper, you just never know."

"Mother, tell me everything you know about Robbie."

Without questioning, Mother began relating the story about Robbie, how Johnny and VanderHaar had brought him here, how they were to pretend it was their grandson, how VanderHaar was executed shortly after, how Johnny had to go into hiding, and how Franz and Albert were fond of the little boy; if only they knew it was a Jew. How Anna had taken Robbie completely under her wing, as though it was her own child, and how he stole everyone's heart.

"But Mother, did Robbie come with anything of his own?"

"Yes," Mother answered, still not knowing where Agnes was going with all this information, "he came wrapped in a soft embroidered blanket with his name on it."

"Do you still have it?"

"Of course. I kept it."

"Can I see it?"

"How about tomorrow? I don't want to wake anyone."

"Please, Mother," Agnes begged, and began explaining why it was so important for her to see it.

Mother quietly left the room. The silence in the house remained unbroken. Agnes waited for what seemed a long time, but finally Mother returned, in her hands a soft embroidered blanket with the name "Robbie" on it.

She quietly handed Agnes the blanket. The dim light in the room was enough to see the colors and the precision of the embroidery. Agnes softly traced the letters with her fingers.

"Mother, his parents have been hiding with us for the past two years."

"We have been hiding the same family?" Mother whispered in awe. Her hand found Agnes's hand resting on the arm of the chair. They sat together, wrapped in the soft silence of the night, enveloped by a sense of awe, mesmerized by what seemed a true miracle, Agnes still softly caressing the letters embroidered on the blanket—Robbie.

MOMENT OF TRUTH

Nikko disappeared for a few days. In the hut, everything seemed normal. Plans were made to prepare for the dropping of food, and idle time was passed with games of chess, conversation, and going for short walks one at a time.

Breakfast at Dora's was the highlight of the day. Johnny was waiting for Nikko. He stayed close to Bart. He observed his every movement, listened to every word he said, but besides the slight stoop in his right shoulder, nothing revealed that Bart had anything to hide from the others.

Johnny began questioning the truth about him. "Maybe he was just fine. Maybe he had nothing to hide. Maybe he just went for a walk that early morning. But why was Bart gone for so long? Is Bart aware that he is shadowed so closely?" His thoughts wandered off to Lisa. He felt his strength returning. Her presence gave him a sense of courage. Her eyes had touched his soul deeply, and even though she might be relating messages throughout the network at this very moment, he felt her presence with him, wondering if she was feeling the same way.

He joined in with the light conversation of the men. Always praising Dora's coffee, Dora's pancakes, and jokingly discussing the "farm work" for the day ahead. Some of them actually did help out from time to time.

"Nikko," Dora announced, "I knew you would join. Saved you some pancakes, please eat." Nikko had entered the kitchen quietly. Johnny was still fixed on Bart's facial expression, but there was no noticeable change, nothing that gave him away as being a betrayer. Johnny did detect, however, a slight raising of his right shoulder, intensifying the stoop by just an inch. Johnny imitated the movement to feel for himself whether this gesture could be an expression of fear or uneasiness. He decided it could, but that this would never be enough proof for his accusation. Nikko's eyes met Johnny's. He clearly had something to tell him. When finally, all the men left, Nikko said he would join later. He wanted to enjoy more pancakes. Johnny lingered and when it was clear no one was around, he took his seat beside Nikko.

"And?" Johnny whispered.

Dora was washing the dishes, making enough noise to give them some privacy to talk.

"It has to happen today."

"What?"

"We have to take care of Bart today."

"What proof do you have?"

"It is an order. No details now. Please trust."

"How and when, who, where?" Johnny panicked. He did not want to be involved in this. Every cell in his body resisted. He could not kill another man.

"What proof?"

"Trust this decision. If we don't do it now, more people will die. This whole village will be in trouble. The Nazis will retaliate."

"Who is going to do it?"

"I will," Nikko said calmly.

Nikko explained his plan. Johnny had to inform the men in the next hour. He had to be extremely cautious.

"I will be there at 6:30 in the early evening and ask Bart to come with me for a brief walk. You will lead the men into promising that nobody will ever talk about this incident, after which you will all come out and encircle us. I will pull the trigger."

Nikko noticed Johnny's face turning pale. He realized that this was asking almost the impossible from Johnny.

"You step about thirty yards outside the circle and keep watch for all of us. When it is safe, you use your famous bird whistle."

Johnny visibly relaxed. He forced a smile and for a moment, thought of Lisa. The warmth of her eyes gave him strength. He thought of Dora, of his family, of all the people who were involved in the network. Everyone was in danger by this one betrayer, who was trying to make money from it all. He thought of VanderHaar. Nikko was right; this had to happen.

"Thanks, Nikko, I will do what is needed."

Nikko hugged him.

"I know I can count on you, Johnny."

Together they walked across the moor to the hut.

"You go in first, Johnny. I'll be there shortly."

Bart seemed deeply fixed on his next move in his game of chess. Nikko followed shortly thereafter. He walked right up to Bart. Johnny overheard the conversation. Bart was not willing to leave his game of chess. He almost won the game, he uttered.

"It's just a game. This is important; you can go back to it soon," Nikko bluffed. Bart resisted even more. When Nikko pulled his revolver from his pocket and pointed it at him, he dropped his resistance and got up to go with Nikko.

"Sorry, Bart, it doesn't look like you are going to win this game."

They walked out.

Everyone in the hut was astonished. Johnny took the lead. He quickly explained what had happened.

"We will all take responsibility for this act." They stood close in a circle and held their right hands together. "We hereby swear that no one will ever know about the killing of Bart."

"Now we have to go out. Nikko is waiting."

Nikko stood in the open clearing, the same place where the men had collected weapons from the British planes that had flown over to help the Resistance. His revolver pointed at Bart, who stood there defiantly yet afraid of what was about to happen. Bart refused to confess and claimed innocence.

The men formed a circle around him.

"Buter, go to your post. Make sure we are safe," Nikko ordered.

Johnny left with a heavy heart. He threw one look at Bart, one shoulder raised more than ever. The same gesture that gave him away a few nights ago when he was making his way out of the hut to betray their plans for the food dropping. "Was he?" Johnny would never know for sure.

It was dark and utterly still. Johnny checked the surroundings. He didn't spot anything suspicious. He curled his thumb and index finger and brought them to his mouth. His bird whistle trailed off across the moor, ensuring his team that everything was safe.

In the distance he heard a muffled shot. It was all over. He stayed on his post for a while. His stomach turned. Anger welled up. Anger at war, at injustice, at his own inability to make any changes. Finally, he ran to the hut. He wanted to hide in his sleeping bag. He was the first to enter. The men must still be out there cleaning up the mess. The game of chess was left untouched. He walked over to the board and carefully studied the set up. One more move, and Bart would have won the game. He slowly raised his arm and swept the pieces off the board. At that same moment, Nikko entered followed by the men. Nikko walked up to him. They looked at the fallen chess pieces chaotically spread out on the floor.

"In war, nobody really wins," Johnny finally broke the silence. Nikko nodded solemnly in agreement. The men huddled, sticking together, knowing that this secret would follow them for the rest of their lives.

Joy

The ride home was a lot easier than last time. Her bags were once again stuffed with food and goodies. The most precious gift of all, though, was the colorful embroidered blanket with the name "Robbie" gracefully written on it. Still in awe of the miracle she was experiencing, she pushed the pedals with all her might, so she could be home before evening. Agnes was eager to share this happy news. She had left the house very early. Mother had prepared the food and packed her bags. She carried the blanket on her body under her warm winter coat, just in case she might lose the bags.

"Let's hope this war ends soon," were Mother's last words. Agnes was filled with hope. If this could happen, then why could this war not end? With one-pointed focus she pedaled on with a steady rhythm, determined that nothing could stop her. Time disappeared.

She finally reached Amsterdam. In half an hour she should be home. For a moment, she relished her time alone, the cold night air, unaware of the pain in her body from the long ride, experiencing pure joy. For a moment she realized that her petty self was but a small aspect of who she really was, and that everyone's petty self was truly only a very small aspect of who they truly were. She realized her own courage, and she realized the courage in everyone else. She realized the power of love, and her state became even more elated. She kept on riding and finally reached her house.

They were all waiting for her. Henk took the bags, and started to unpack. Robbie jumped on her lap and hugged her closely. Edith and Mark were sitting at the table, tense, holding back in anticipation of what news they might hear.

Agnes unbuttoned her heavy coat, and from underneath she gently pulled out the blanket with the colorful embroidery.

Edith walked up to her. She took it with both hands and began caressing Robbie's embroidered name. Tears were streaming down her cheeks. Mark gently folded her into his arms. Together they held the blanket as though they were holding their own little Robbie himself.

Agnes and Henk watched in silence. The room filled with joy. Henk set the table, and soon they were celebrating the great news.

The food lasted a couple of weeks before once again, hunger struck. As food got scarce again, the tension in the house increased.

CLOSE TO FREEDOM

There were the early signs of spring. Bird song and tiny buds, promising that life would soon be there once again, abundant and lush. The men had gathered in the hut. They bent over the small radio that was, surprisingly, still functioning on the same batteries it started with many months ago. The reception was poor, and they had to strain to hear the words that were said on Radio Orange, but one thing was clear: freedom was on its way. The Germans admitted a boat from Sweden with food to the west of Holland. Americans, Canadians, and English Allies were allowed to drop food packets over Amsterdam. Russia had pushed the Germans back all the way to the German border. The south of Holland was completely free, and slowly other towns followed. It wouldn't be long before the north too would experience freedom.

"We are almost there," Nikko said, "but we can't slacken, the Germans are still in power, and they seem more vicious than ever. The Nazis have destroyed many bridges so far, to prevent the Allies from coming through. We must protect our bridge in the village."

Together they came up with a plan. They were to take turns watching the Germans closely from the houses along the bridge, relieving each other as needed. The plan worked. Johnny found himself in an attic of one of the houses right by the bridge. He saw Germans checking out the bridge.

It soon became clear that this bridge too was a target for the Germans. Something had to be done soon. They made a plan. All the men went to the bridge. They crept up from different directions and joined some of the local forces planning for an attack. When the command came, everyone began shooting at the German Nazis. Some were killed, and the others ran for dear life, but the bridge did not survive. Johnny did not agree with this mission. Who would have to pay for this in the end? The bridge was blown up anyway. What did we gain by this? He ran back over the moors to the hut. In due time the others joined him. They all agreed, this was a reckless move. Nikko too was upset with the commander in charge of this mission. He should have waited. At least five Germans were killed. They were bound to take revenge.

They were right. Mara was the first to bring the news. Fifty villagers were kept prisoners, including women and children. At the same time, rumors had it that the Allies were coming closer.

"We need your help." Mara brought the message but could tell there was very little that could be done, if they wanted to save the lives of their people.

"We must go and fight," Nikko said, "and take the weapons."

They were not the only ones arriving at the canal. Villagers, soldiers, everyone was ready to fight. The Germans had returned, and it turned out to be a terrible battle, until helicopters circled and big tanks arrived.

"The Allies, the Allies, they are here!" everyone started screaming. The Germans fled, and bit by bit they let go of their hostages, who returned frightened, but luckily, unharmed.

AN UNEXPECTED VISIT

Agnes had made another visit to the community kitchen. She had to wait in line for hours, only to come home again with a pot of watery soup made from potatoes and onions. This had become their usual routine. Agnes was considering another trip east, but Henk told her to wait. The war should end soon. All the signs were there. They were sitting together at the dinner table in the kitchen, eating the soup Agnes had fetched from the soup stand. Their conversation was minimal, and the tension was high. All of a sudden, they were startled by the sound of a car stopping abruptly in front of their house. Henk walked over to the front room and peeked through the curtains. He noticed that a German jeep had pulled up right in front of their house.

"Clear the table, quickly!" he commanded Agnes.

"Edith, Mark, go upstairs," he urged, trying not to give in to the panic that took hold of him.

The bell rang. Henk didn't answer. The bell rang again. This time longer and louder it seemed. Henk took a deep breath and tried to regain his calm. When Edith and Mark were out of sight, and the dishes were removed from the table, Henk slowly opened the door.

"Guten Abend," one of the German soldiers spoke with a smile on his face. Henk was surprised.

"We are Franz and Albert, we stay in your grandparents's school. Your mother has been delightful to us. She knew we were going to Amsterdam and gave us these bags with food. She thought you could use them."

Henk took the bags, not knowing what to say. He tried to act normal.

"Your son is doing well. He is getting stronger by the day. You'll have him back before you know it. *Alles Guten."* And with that, they left.

Agnes came out of the kitchen, Robbie behind her skirt.

"Good thing they didn't see Robbie," Henk said as he handed her the bags with food. Edith and Mark came down the stairs. They looked at the bags with food, they looked at Robbie, they looked at each other, and when they realized everyone was safe, they burst out laughing. Soon the table was reset, food was shared, and everyone was once again in good spirits.

"This must be a sign the war is ending," Agnes said hopefully.

LIBERATION

April 6, East of Holland. Big tanks entered the small village streets. People were out, singing, dancing, and hugging. The Canadian Allies entered the town as heroes. They handed chocolate and chewing gum to all the villagers. Benevolent smiles, heroic gestures, and euphoria was everywhere. Johnny and Lisa joined hands and followed one of the tanks. Each of them was waving a flag and wearing orange, amidst an orange crowd waving red, white, and blue flags. Songs of freedom, tears of happiness and relief filled the air.

Those who fought on the side of the Germans fled the country. Freedom had finally come.

May 4, Amsterdam. Radio news: Negotiations between the Allied Forces and the Germans are taking place. Food transport is opened. Marshall Montgomery has officially accepted the surrender of the Germans.

"We are so close to freedom," Henk shared, "but still we have to be careful. Even though the Germans have officially surrendered, technically the Germans are still here, and they still have the power to do what they want. We shall stay inside, until we know for sure."

May 5, Amsterdam. Radio news: A second treaty of surrender has been signed in Hotel de Wereld in Wageningen. The Netherlands is now a free country again.

"We have to stay in till the Allies come. Europe is free, but the Nazis are still here," Henk announced.

"I've heard that many of them are fleeing, and so are the Dutch traitors. The camps too have been freed. People are coming back!" Agnes shared the rumors she had heard while waiting in line for the community kitchen.

May 7, Amsterdam. People couldn't hold their joy any longer. Thousands of people went out to the streets, singing, dancing, hugging, and crying tears of intense relief. Masses of red, white, blue, and orange filled the streets of Amsterdam.

"We are staying put," Henk urged Agnes and his guests. "The Allies are still not here yet."

May 7. Radio news: Nazis shot into the crowd for two hours on Dam Square from a nearby rooftop. More than a hundred people were wounded and at least thirty-two civilians were killed.

"Why now? The treaties for peace have been signed," Edith wondered in despair. "Will it ever stop?"

More Radio news: Tanks are entering Amsterdam. Finally, the city is free. More and more people are joining the crowds, celebrating their freedom.

"Let's go." Mark took Edith by the arm, and together they ran out to the street. For the first time, after two long, dark years of hiding, they experienced fresh air and freedom. They danced out onto the streets, followed by Henk and Agnes, carrying Robbie on her arm.

Masses of tanks moved through the streets. Everywhere people were singing and waving their flags. The Allies handed out chocolates, chewing gum, and cigarettes.

Amsterdam was free. It wouldn't take long before the whole country would be free.

Reunion

"Okay, baby brother, you and I are going to make a big trip," Anna told Robbie, as she was helping him dress in his most beautiful clothes. "The war is over, and you are going to be back to your own parents."

"Grandpa and grandma my parents," he cried out.

"No, Grandpa and grandma are my parents," Anna tried to explain. Anna took him in her lap and held him closely to her heart. She had come to love Robbie as though he was her own child. Now that the war was over, plans were made to bring Robbie back to his own parents. Anna was to go with him for the first six months, so Robbie could get used to his new home. Anna was excited to go to Amsterdam and to be able to stay with Robbie for a while longer. It was a great adventure for her too, because she had barely left her own village.

"Robbie, I'm going with you for a long time," she tried to prepare him for his farewell. "Everyone here is going to miss you, Robbie. Everyone here loves you."

Robbie was enjoying the attention and looked at her with his big smiling eyes.

"Robbie love Anna."

The next day, Robbie was the center of attention. Everyone showered love on him, and they were all sad he was leaving. Even Father took him in his lap.

"Now, you be a good boy when you are back with your mom and dad," Father lectured him with his usual schoolteacher's voice. Robbie was taking it all in, not really knowing what was in store for him.

Johnny lifted Robbie as high as he could. Robbie was screeching with joy. He looked the little boy in the eyes. He felt a rush of gratitude and love for all the people who had helped Robbie to be safe. He thought of VanderHaar and Lisa. He realized that Robbie had been the key to his work in the Resistance with Nikko, and also how Robbie had been instrumental in bringing Lisa into his life. The girl with the braids, whom he admired and loved so much. He thought of the miracle of the embroidered blanket. He thought of Swan.

"Do what you have to do, trust."

He carefully put Robbie back on his feet, then took his hands, and swung him around like a carousel.

"Put him down, Johnny, we want Robbie home in one piece," Mother worried. Johnny gave Robbie one more tight hug.

"I'll come and see you as often as I can," he told him.

Everyone was taking their time saying goodbye to Robbie.

Early the next morning, a car pulled up in front of the house. Anna and Robbie were all ready to go. Johnny and Joop loaded their suitcases into the car. Mara put her arm around Anna, kissing her goodbye one more time. Father and Mother each held Robbie's hand as Robbie was swinging in between them.

The car started. Lots of hands were waving till Robbie and Anna were out of sight.

"The war is over," Father said, as they turned back to the house. "Let's move on and live our lives."

That was Father. Johnny admired him for his steadfastness and his strength. He went to his room. He found Jerry buried in his books.

"Still studying, Jerry?" Johnny asked in disbelief.

"I want to pass my exam for law school," Jerry answered. "What are you planning to do, Johnny?"

"I have no idea," Johnny responded.

"Go on and finish high school," Jerry encouraged him.

But Johnny didn't show the slightest desire to go back to school.

"What is there to learn, after all we have gone through?"

Jerry gave up and bent his head over his books once again.

*   *   *

The car stopped in one of the streets in Amsterdam. Anna and Robbie were excited by everything they saw. Many people on the streets, lots of cars, tall houses, narrow sidewalks, a life so different from their own. The car came to a stop. A lady stepped out of one of the doors, as though she had been on the lookout and knew they were coming. Before the car even came to a complete stop, she opened the door on Robbie's side. She took Robbie in her arms. She cried, and cried, "Robbie, you are back, my dear, dear Robbie." With Robbie in her arms, she kissed Anna and invited her in. Mark welcomed them both. They became a happy family. Sorrows from the past seemingly dissolved. The joy of having their own Robbie back temporarily replaced the sadness over the people who never returned. Edith took out the blanket and caressed her mother's embroidered letters.

"Will she ever see Robbie?"

"Will she ever come back?"

It was her love that made this miracle happen.

"Mother," she whispered softly, "please, return."

FAREWELL

"Johnny, a letter for you!" Mother yelled outside, while Johnny was tinkering on an old car, trying to make it work. It had been sitting around for years, and no one had been able to get it fixed nor been interested. Johnny was just looking for something to do. Everyone else seemed to get on with life, as though the war had never happened. How could they forget so easily? How could they worry about Jerry's test results, Mara's plans to go back to school, and about what's for lunch tomorrow? Anna's letters were equally superficial. "Robbie is doing well, his parents are wonderful people, and she is having the time of her life, getting to know the big city." Did they forget what had just happened?

"Johnny, a letter. It is from the government!" Mother yelled outside again. Johnny abandoned the old rusty car and walked back to the house. Mother handed him the letter.

"Aren't you going to open it?" she said impatiently, urging him to read what she believed to be an important letter from the government. He pulled one of his tools from his pocket and carefully slit open the envelope.

While reading the letter, his face broke out into a big smile.

"What is it, Johnny? An acknowledgement?"

"More than that, Mom, an invitation to join the Marines going to America for training at Camp David, fighting the Japanese in Indonesia. The war may be over here, but this is a World War, and there is more work to do."

"But Johnny, why would you volunteer to go to war. The war is over, you have a life ahead of you. Please, don't go, Johnny; that will be your death. You have a life here; you have done enough for our country."

Lisa came outside. She overheard the last sentence and wanted to know what was going on. She had grown fond of Johnny and was silently hoping the two of them could continue to see each other and build their friendship. She had also noticed Johnny's listlessness. She noticed he couldn't find his place anymore. He told her about the invitation to go to America.

"They are recruiting you, Johnny. I'd rather you stay," she tried to convince him, but also realized she should give him time to make his own decision. After a moment of silence, she added, "I'll finish nursing school, and I'll wait for you."

He looked her in the eyes and saw the same penetrating eyes, full of determination, revealing the strength he had admired when he first met her on the boat, and later in Dora's kitchen.

"I will be back, believe me."

"I'll take you to Rotterdam and will send you off."

Epilogue

You may wonder, what happened to Johnny, what happened to Robbie? You may wonder if this story is based on a true story, which events happened for real, and which are fiction? You may wonder about the author, and why she wanted to write this story.

I wrote the story because it is a story of my family—it is the story of my father, "Johnny."

My grandfather, the headmaster of the school, was married with two children, Henk and Louis. Their mother died from the Spanish flu and left my grandfather with the kids. Henk studied to become a teacher, and later moved to Amsterdam. Louis moved to the States.

My grandfather (Father) remarried with my grandmother (Mother), and from that marriage came: Gerrit (Jerry), the lawyer who needed his books while hiding); Johan (Johnny), who you know; Annie (who took care of Robbie); Marg (Mara), who was also deeply involved in the resistance; and Jan (Joop) who was the youngest and proud to help out in his own way.

So Henk was the half-brother of Johnny. It turned out that Henk and his wife had a son called Robbie, who was of the same age as Agnes's son. A total coincidence. So there really were two Robbie's.

As I was growing up, my father told me bits and pieces about his experiences in World War II and about the time he spent in the war between The Netherlands and Indonesia. He wanted to forget the nine years of living in war. It was mostly a closed chapter in his life.

Johnny married my mother and had three children. My brother was born a year after my father returned from Indonesia. I was born four years later, and seven years later, my younger sister was born.

As a child, I had a very close relationship with my dad. He had become a teacher, and besides teaching math, he taught me life lessons that have stayed with me to this day. His number one value was that you had to be able to keep a secret. You had to be able to not give away any secret, under any circumstances. He also was a man of his word. He would never break a promise. You could rely on him. He still loved adventure and as a family, we went out on great camping trips, discovering new places in Europe every summer.

I did ask him about the war from time to time. I wondered if he had ever killed someone. I still remember his face upon that question. He didn't give me an answer straight away. He had to think before he said no. It wasn't until after his death that a family friend called us and relayed a message from my father that he was asked to keep secret all those years. That's when we learned that he indeed was involved in the execution of the betrayer in their group during the Resistance. He was not the one pulling the trigger, but all the men had taken full responsibility for this deed and promised to never mention it thereafter. I remember when I was in high school asking him if he agreed with the death penalty, as they did in the United States. I didn't expect his strong reaction. He was fully opposed to it because, he said, you never knew one hundred percent for sure if the person had indeed committed the crime. It wasn't until later that I realized he had carried that guilt inside him his whole life. After all, he had promised not to speak about it, so he kept it inside. We were lucky he at least confided in one friend.

When I was a teenager, life took a turn. My brother had already left home, and my sister was still in her elementary school years. I feel like that's when I lost my father. He changed, he became depressed and very angry at times. At the time, none of us knew about post-traumatic war syndrome. We couldn't explain it. My father left to live in his hometown, back in the east of Holland. My parents divorced, and we all went our own way. At times when I did visit my dad, he took me to the moors and showed me where the hut was. He talked about the war then. He also took me to the farm where they got their food, and where people were hiding during the war. I was amazed at the friendliness of the people there, people I had never met before, and their coffee was indeed delicious.

But at that time, I still didn't understand why our family life had to fall apart so drastically. I spent many years trying to find out, getting more stories, and I finally realized that participating in a war, no matter what side anyone is on, is detrimental for any human being. When my father was in Indonesia, I learned that he very soon realized he was fighting an unjust war. He didn't want to be there. Luckily, he was working with the cars, because he was a good mechanic, but only recently the horrors that took place during that time have become public knowledge. No one remains unchanged after witnessing violence.

The slogan "Never Again" is, for most people in Europe, a sacred vow. Even though there hasn't been a war to that extent, looking around the world, wars are raging everywhere. People are suffering from war, not only now; their lives will be affected long past the actual events. Every story has a lesson for the future. Is this story going to solve wars? No, but in looking at my own life, I can decide to be kinder to others, to have compassion for others, and to contribute to a peaceful world that way.

My brother and I used to have conversations about the war. The one question, "What would you do?" always came up. I don't know what I would have done in the situation my grandparents, my aunts and uncles, and my father were in. I do know that I have a lot of respect for all the people who placed their own lives in danger in order to save others, in order to serve justice.

As far as Robbie, who was hidden with my family during the war, that too is a true story. Robbie agreed that I could use his real name. All the other names are made up. It was truly a miracle that parents and son were hiding with the same family, not knowing until almost the end of the war. Even though Robbie was very young when all this happened, the war certainly has left deep scars in his life. But he seems to be a happy father and grandfather. His mother passed away after living a long life, and they were very close. I only met her when I was a child, and I remember her kindness. She remained very close to my aunt, who stayed with Robbie the first six months after the war, so he could get used to his "new" family in Amsterdam.

Robbie has written his own story about his life, also with the intention of spreading the message of "Never Again." I made up the girl with the braids. I wanted a girl in there that was meaningful to Johnny, perhaps as my way of coming to terms with the separation between my parents. The two trips on the bicycle during the Hunger Winter truly happened. I never understood how my aunt did it, but during those days, women displayed immense courage. They made those trips. I made up the family she spent the night with. But it could have happened, as it happened all the time. And, believe it or not, the fishing really happened.

It is true that I had to fill in many gaps. Some I filled in with research, some by talking to other people who were in similar situations, some by using my own imagination. We can never truly look into anyone's soul, and therefore an author gives away parts of his or her own soul, because the truth is we are not all that different from each other. Each of us carries the collective knowledge we hold as humans, inside. However, if any of the characters, or friends or family, represented in this story feels that this story is not doing true justice to their experience of that time during the war, please forgive me. Know that it is fiction based on a true story, and the intention of the story is to tell of a time belonging to a people, many of whom are no longer walking this earth, so that we, and those who will be walking this earth in the future, may never forget.

For me personally, it is also a tribute to my father and his family, and to the Jewish family hiding through the war, and for the legacy they left me of finding my way to contribute to a world of "Never Again." Just as the embroidered blanket, made with so much love, was ultimately the reason Robbie and his parents found each other, so I believe that every act of love will contribute to a greater harmony in our world.

Almost seventy years after the fact, Johanna, my cousin, and Alef, my brother, represented my aunt and uncle, and my grandparents, when receiving the honorary award from Yad Vashem, an Israeli organization honoring all people who have put their lives at risk in order to save the Jews during World War II. Rob's—the boy who was hiding with my grandparents—request was approved. Those who stood up for justice never thought of any kind of reward, yet those who received the legacy are humbled to stand in their place, honoring their remarkable lives of courage.